JUDGE FRANKENSTEIN

MERCY OVER JUDGEMENT
BOOK TWO

CHRISTOPHER D. TAYLOR

Wise Path Books
12407 N Mopac Expy #250
Austin, TX 78758

ISBNs:
978-1-969924-99-6 (paperback)
978-1-969924-23-1 (ebook)

CONTENTS

At that time Jesus said, "I praise you Father, Lord of heaven and earth, because you have hidden these things from the wise and learned, and revealed them to little children. Yes, Father, for this is what you were pleased to do." — Matthew 11:25-26

1

UPSTAIRS

The six-year-old sat at his school lunch table sipping a grape soda. It was Friday. Presently, the boy remembered his parents were taking him to Grandpa and Wemaw's house tonight. He smiled. He liked going to his grandparents' house. He remembered the last time he was there; it was cold. There were leaves on the ground. Sammy remembered and visualized Wemaw pushing him in a swing followed by Grandpa tossing a football with him. Then he visualized grabbing that football and diving into a plush bed of raked autumn leaves. "That was fun," he thought.

That night, after a three-hour drive, the family of three arrived in Poplarton, Texas. It was late, but Sammy ran toward his grandparents as Grandpa proclaimed, "There's my number one grandson!" As Grandpa embraced him, Sampson Phillip Marshall noticed something he had never seen before. Sammy saw a subtle mark on Grandpa's hand that began where his thumb met his palm. The faint line extended downward past his wrist and traveled onto his forearm. After the gleeful hugs and brief inquiries about the drive, Sammy was headed for bed. He really liked going to his grandparents' house, but at night the house frightened him. It was old. It made spooky noises. For example, there was a large staircase to the second floor, and every step, every single step creaked. At the base of the staircase stood an ornate grandfather clock that seemed to wait until Sammy arrived to let loose its haunting gongs. It seemed to him that the grandfather clock gonged even louder when he was alone and vulnerable.

Sammy's limited experience with the stairwell provided him with a plan. He knew that if he could run past the grandfather clock and climb the steep, creaky stairs without perishing, he would encounter something even scarier. At the top of the first flight of stairs was a landing situated several feet above the top of the menacing clock. For some reason never known to Sammy, his grandparents hung a painting on the wall that depicted an old, bearded man with a patch over his right eye. Presuming that the old man let him pass without popping out of that painting to destroy him, Sammy could then proceed up the remaining five steps (the creakiest of them all), arriving at a place called "the upstairs." Upstairs. That's how the family referred to the second floor of the house. Upstairs. From Sammy's perspective, the name alone was foreboding.

The entryway to the upstairs at the top of the stairwell consisted of a closed door. When Sammy twisted the black handle, the door would suddenly pop open with ease. It seemed that "the upstairs" knew of his arrival, welcoming him in. But welcoming him in... to what? There were four bedrooms upstairs and one bathroom. Except for the constantly creaking floors, it was quiet up there. Very quiet. Much like the opportunistic grandfather clock, it seemed to Sammy's six-year-old mind that the upstairs was just waiting to get him alone. He believed that the upstairs relished the thought of all his loving family members remaining down there while he stayed up here. Because the upstairs was just waiting for that to happen, that was the scenario Sammy feared the most—being alone … upstairs.

So, Sammy let out a sigh and smiled that night when his mother, Sarah Marshall, told him that he would not be going to bed upstairs alone. The procedure that night consisted of the following events. Sammy hopped into Grandpa and Wemaw's bed. Grandpa, otherwise known as Taylor O'Connell, wished him a good night's sleep and then read a book under the only source of light in the room: a lamp on a bedside table. As Grandpa read, Sammy fell asleep. Sarah and Wemaw, otherwise known as Francis O'Connell, visited for hours, but Sammy's dad, Phil Marshall, made his way upstairs to find Sammy fast asleep in his grandparents' bed. No longer alone. Beloved. Sammy woke up the next morning in the adjacent bedroom occupied by his parents. He never knew how he got there, but suspected his dad had something to do with it.

The next day was a glorious Saturday. Sammy had a new baseball and a new glove, so he begged for a game of catch with his dad and grandfather. Sammy, Phil and Grandpa threw around a baseball on the dewy green grass with towering trees interspersed between them. It never dawned on Sammy that he was the only one with a glove, but his dad and Grandpa steadily endured the pain of the game. After fifteen minutes, Phil excused himself to take a shower, leaving Sammy and Grandpa to play catch a few minutes longer. There would be many more games of catch between the boy and Grandpa. Sometimes it was a baseball. Sometimes it was a football. Grandpa never complained about not having a glove or Sammy's occasional errant throw. He was pleased to spend time with his grandson. On one occasion, Sammy arrived without bringing a ball of any sort. When he voiced his disappointment over this oversight, Grandpa found a large pinecone in the yard. Grandpa and grandson then threw it back and forth to one another. The day was saved, but their hands hurt afterward.

AFTER A FUN-FILLED Saturday with his parents and grandparents, Sammy was given a daunting task. The whole family was downstairs in the kitchen when his mother said to him, "Sammy, sweetie, run upstairs and get your dress shoes. Dad wants to spiff them up a bit before church tomorrow. Remember, you stepped in the mud last week?"

He gulped hard. "Ok, momma, where are they?"

"Under our bed where you slept last night. Go on, please."

He began to run toward the staircase as he realized her specific instructions were to go upstairs BY HIMSELF and then reach UNDER THE BED for his shoes. Was his mom not familiar with haunted houses? Did she not know how they worked? Surely, he had no chance of survival. "I'll never see her again," he thought as he accelerated past the tick-tock of the grandfather clock. When he reached the stairs, he looked up at the landing ahead. "No," he thought. "Don't look! Don't look at him!" As the brave boy ran toward the grimacing eye-patched ghoul in the painting, he could feel an icy hand extend toward him as he shuddered, running by as fast as he could. Sammy could feel his own heartbeat now as he entered the upstairs by twisting the handle of the closed portal, and suddenly all was silent. He was there. Alone. "I'm brave. I must be brave," he uttered under his breath. The floor below gave a resounding creak with each step he took toward what seemed like certain doom.

He entered the guest bedroom, and reached under the bed as fast as he could. He grabbed something with a handle. "Oh no!" he thought. "Shoes don't have handles!" He briefly considered taking whatever the handled object was to his mother, claiming ignorance. "Surely she would like to have this...umbrella. No, be brave. Look, don't just reach!" Sammy closed one eye, looking under the bed with the other. Thankfully, he saw no demons. He saw no evil of any kind. There! On the far left sat his dress shoes. He grabbed them and retraced his steps. He was back downstairs instantly but received a mild scolding for running down the stairs. "That's dangerous!" said Wemaw. Soon after his quick apology, Sammy presented his shoes to his dad. Through deep breaths, he said, "Dad, I went up to the upstairs by myself. It was scary, but I'm okay."

Phil smiled and tussled his son's hair. "Good job, son. You're a brave boy."

Several minutes later, Sammy heard Grandpa say, "Sammy, you are a fast runner! You breezed right by me upstairs! I don't think you knew I was there!"

"You were there?"

"Yes! I was in my room reading. You were quick as a cat!"

The six-year-old became relieved but disappointed. He instantly processed the realization that he wasn't alone after all. His grandfather was in the upstairs with him.

A part of him was glad he wasn't alone. Another part of him felt like his accomplishment was now diminished. For some reason, he wished he had done it himself on his own.

After church on Sunday, Sammy, Phil, and Sarah said their sad goodbyes to the grandparents, before departing for home. Grandpa's mind slowly shifted toward his duties on Monday. Although Sammy knew nothing of it, his grandfather actually had a job. Taylor O'Connell would get up early the next morning. As the sun rose, he bent his knee, praying that he would do a good job in the sight of the Lord.

2

THE SCAR

Mr. Henry Phipps pulled his car into the parking lot of the Wilson County Courthouse and parked. "Ok, Manny, let's go." Emmanuel Ortega opened the front passenger door. As he walked, he noticed his legs were trembling. The eleven-year-old orphan was summoned to court as a criminal defendant. A fellow orphan named Lucas had dared him to steal a twelve-pack of Coors Light from the 7-11 on the corner of Webb and 9th Street. Lucas had failed to mention that the store had seven security cameras that produced high-quality video surveillance.

Manny wasn't arrested, but he was given a citation for Theft Under $100 by a local detective who gave him a summons to that day's teen court proceeding. Manny entered the courtroom, which was large and cavernous. He could hear his shoes as each step echoed loudly around the ancient room. Mr. Phipps, the chief administrator from the orphanage, said, "Ok, here's our spot to sit and wait. Have a seat."

Manny sat down, waiting for his name to be called. He could feel his heart beating now. His chest felt like it did after running a relay race. He was ashamed. He was afraid. "How could I be so stupid?" he thought. "I'm a typical orphan kid about to have a criminal record. Why did I listen to Lucas? He's an idiot." After a few seconds' pause, he said to himself, "I'm an idiot."

Suddenly, Manny was startled by the booming voice of the bailiff, who bellowed, "All rise!" The back door opened as the judge entered the courtroom. Manny's eyes widened as the older man appeared just as Manny imagined him. The long black robe. The grey hair. The frowny disapproving face. Manny wanted to run and hide. He was terrified now. The thought of standing before this mean judge to answer for his crime filled him with dread. To Manny's eye, even Mr. Phipps appeared uncomfortable, even though he had done nothing wrong.

The judge sat down on his elevated platform, peering down at Manny and all the other kid criminals. To Manny's great surprise, the judge's voice didn't sound mean. He told the crowd to approach the bench when their name was called. Manny presumed that he was supposed to come and stand before the judge, even though he could see no "bench." Thankfully for Manny, his last name was Ortega, so he was able to watch the proceedings as they played out for those whose last names came within the first half of the alphabet. When Manny heard the judge say "Emmanuel Ortega," he knew just what to do. As he stood up, though, his legs seemed unwilling to work as normal. He had to make each footstep toward the terrible judge. Again, he could hear his shoes clap against the old wooden floor. His heart thumped. His ears could hear each breath. "Oh, I hate Lucas!" he thought.

After Manny traveled the necessary thirty feet from his seat, he arrived in front of the judge. Then things got worse. As he saw the judge pick up his file, the black robe revealed something scary. Manny saw a mark on the man's hand that ran from the intersection of his palm and his thumb across the wrist onto his upper forearm. "Judge Frankenstein," shuddered Manny.

"Mr. Ortega," the judge began.

"You have the right to..." and that's all. That's all Manny could take in. The stress of the situation and the big legal words used by Judge Frankenstein caused Manny to panic. His trance of escape suddenly ended as Mr. Phipps nudged him. "Do you understand the judge? Is that what you want to do? I think it's your best option." Manny involuntarily nodded his head and said, "Yeah."

The judge's long, pointy finger directed Manny to a signature line where he shakily scribbled his name. Manny endured a brief lecture from the robed figure. Manny managed a faint "thank you" as Mr. Phipps took his elbow, leading him away from the judge. It was over. He survived. "I'll never break the law again," thought he. Manny was then informed by a clerk that he had the chance to clear his name. "Because you are so young, the law offers you the chance to keep this charge off of your permanent criminal record. Do you understand, Mr. Ortega?" "Yes," he affirmed.

"The judge has sentenced you to forty hours of community service to be performed within the next ninety days. As long as you perform your community service within that time, this charge will be dismissed, so it won't go on your record." Manny replied, "Ok, good."

"As the judge told you, theft is one of those charges that you really, really don't want on your record. So, make sure you get your hours done in a timely manner. Bring this form back here once the hours have been completed. Mr. Phipps will help you do that. Won't you, Mr. Phipps?"

"Yes, of course."

When Mr. Phipps and Emmanuel Ortega entered the car,

Mr. Phipps said, "That's a good deal, Manny. Do your hours and clear your record. It will be as if your crime never happened." Manny outwardly replied, "Yes, I will. I don't want to be a thief." Inwardly, he replied, "I'll do anything to stay away from Judge Frankenstein." "I'll do anything," he said under his breath.

The next morning, as was his habit every Tuesday morning, Sammy's grandpa sat down with his teen court docket from the day before. He prayed for each person listed on the page. Sometimes, he would think of a particular interaction with one of the defendants or try to remember each face to make the prayer more personal. On this occasion, he found that his eyes kept returning over and over to the name of Emmanuel Ortega. "Is that name spelled correctly?" he thought. He recalled that Emmanuel Ortega looked particularly frightened. In his heart, Grandpa never wanted to frighten anyone, but knew that sometimes fear was helpful to turn a kid around. As Judge O'Connell looked at the teen docket, he said, "Let's see here, what did Emmanuel do? I can't remember." Then he read the file and thought to himself, "Oh yes, he's the one who stole a twelve-pack of beer from 7-11. Eleven-year-olds don't typically drink beer. It must have been a prank, or a challenge or dare or *tickety tockety*, whatever they call it these days."

He then prayed, "Lord, please bless Emmanuel's life. Oh! Emmanuel. Lord, You must like that name. 'God with us.' May it be so, Lord. Be with Emmanuel. Live through him. And may he live through You. In Christ's name. Amen."

3

HIDING AND MOVING

Over the next few weeks, Manny dutifully performed his assigned community service hours. He was motivated to clear his name, but that was secondary. Mainly, he was motivated to stay away from the courthouse and its monstrous judge. Mr. Phipps took Manny around to the local food pantries, so he could do his work and then return to the orphanage.

On one such occasion, Manny was putting donated cans into a cabinet when he heard a pantry employee say, "Well, good morning, your honor!" Manny looked up. There was Judge Frankenstein entering through the squeaky front door. Manny immediately knelt on the dusty floor behind the tall stack of food cans. He inwardly cursed, "What's HE doing here?! He must have come to check up on me. He's here to make sure I'm doing everything JUST right." He then expressed these inner thoughts out loud, muttering to himself, "Why else would HE be here?"

As he was hiding and muttering, Manny missed the following conversation.

"Jack, I have two months' worth of pantry items this time. I'm sorry, I just didn't have time to come by last month."

"That's okay, Judge! We are always happy to see you and your wife. We are so thankful for your support."

After several seconds of kneeling, Manny peered from behind his refuge in time to see Judge O'Connell squeak the door on his way out. He stood up and sighed with relief. Manny quickly finished his duties. He quickly said his good-byes and entered Mr. Phipps' car before his judge could return to torment him further.

Manny accomplished his forty hours of community service a few weeks later and returned to the courthouse to turn in the form. As soon as Mr. Phipps stopped at the curb, Manny ran as fast as he could into the lobby. He dropped the form into the drop box, barely pausing to do so. He returned to the car unscathed. "Whew!" he said while entering the car. "No sign of that evil judge!"

"Evil? He was really nice to you." After a few seconds, Mr. Phipps' eyebrow furrowed and he continued, "He gave you a way to clear your record. You should be thankful."

"Did you see that scar on his hand and arm?" said Manny. "He is Judge Frankenstein!"

"I don't think you heard a word he said to you. He wanted your good. He was for you. He is a nice man."

"You can believe that if you want. You weren't the one he was after. You weren't the criminal."

Mr. Phipps said, "Thanks to the judge, YOU aren't the criminal either. Your name has been cleared. Think about that."

Manny did think a moment. He thought, "I did the work.

I did the community service. I cleared my name. And now, I don't have to see him again. Never again."

A FEW MONTHS LATER, and many miles north of Manny, Sammy's family made an important decision. On a bright summer morning, Sammy was in his bedroom when he heard a loud engine noise outside. He rushed to his window and saw his dad parking a large moving truck in the driveway. He ran outside filled with excitement, but stopped running abruptly when he saw Phil exit the truck. Sammy stopped running because Phil was suddenly talking with their mailman.

"Hello, Mark. I'm glad I ran into you. Do you have one of those change-of-address forms?"

"Yes sir, I do actually. I guess you found a better place?"

"This has been a good house for us, but we are moving to my wife's hometown in Poplarton."

"Oh, I see," the postman said with a smile. "So, what do you do for a living if you don't mind me asking?"

"Oh, I'm a chemical engineer. I have a new job with an oil company down there. My wife is a family physician taking a new job in Poplarton's main health clinic. It should be a great setup actually. I'll be able to work from home mostly, but will have some overnight travel here and there. We are super close with Sarah's family."

The mailman looked and noticed Sammy standing nearby. "And if you're gone overnight, it will be nice for you all to be near family."

"Yes. We view this move as an answered prayer."

"Well, good luck, sir. Your family will be missed around here."

Phil signed the change of address form before handing it back to the postman. "Thanks very much."

Phil then saw Sammy standing by and said, "Hey champ, want to look inside? Let's check this thing out!" Phil raised the back of the truck and invited Sammy into the large storage trailer. Sarah approached them saying, "Sammy, have you ever been in such a large truck?"

"No way, Mom! Whoa, man! Ha, it echoes my words...do you hear that?" He danced around inside the trailer. "Mom, how far do we live from Wemaw and Grandpa now?"

"About three hours."

"How far will we live from their house in our new house?"

"About ten minutes."

"Mom! That's waaaaay shorter, right?!!"

"Yes! It is much, much shorter."

Phil chimed in. "Sammy, it's like driving from here to your school. That's how short it is."

"Wow, that is super close!!"

In the fall, Sammy was on a new youth soccer team in his new hometown. On a sunny, hot Saturday afternoon, he nearly choked on an orange slice when he saw his grandparents watching from the nearby stands. When the game ended, he ran over to the sidelines, instantly hugged by his dad. Next was Grandpa.

"Great job Sammy!"

"Thanks! Did you see Josh score our goal? He's good!"

"You know what? Josh IS good, but he wouldn't have made that goal if you hadn't made such a great pass to him!"

"Thanks, Grandpa," he replied while giving Wemaw a hug. "I'm so glad you are here!"

"You won't be able to get rid of us, Sammy!" said Wemaw. "We will try to be at everything you do...your sports and school activities. We can't wait!"

Grandpa chimed in, "Yeah! That's why we are so thrilled you live here now. I just hope you don't get tired of seeing us."

"Awesome!! I mean NEVER!"

After Saturday soccer games came Sunday morning church gatherings. Sammy sat between his grandparents at church each Sunday morning as his parents sat next to Wemaw. He felt warm, cared for and affectionately loved as they sang the songs and prayed the prayers together. The church made his family feel at home, and after service, Sammy often heard his grandpa tell another congregant about his most recent athletic or academic accomplishment while placing his hand on Sammy's shoulder. Often the response was, "That's great, Judge. I can see you are proud of him."

4

ORDER IN THE COURT

Sammy entered the 2nd grade that fall. One Saturday when Sammy's soccer team didn't play, Grandpa picked him up, and they went to "the office." Sammy didn't know what that meant, but he would soon find out. Grandpa had some work to do at the courthouse, so he took Sammy along for the first time.

Since it was a Saturday, Sammy and Grandpa were mostly alone in the building. It was a stately edifice filled with wonders for an eight-year-old mind. There was an elevator and a large stairwell. The floor clopped when you walked on it, and all the doors had numbers and looked important. Grandpa unlocked his office and let Sammy sit in his large swivel armchair. He spun around a few times but got up when Grandpa said, "Hey Sammy, come in here!" Sammy ran toward his grandfather's voice, entering the courtroom from the back. He stared in amazement at the largest room he had ever seen. Sammy became overjoyed when Judge O'Connell invited him to take a seat in an even bigger swivel armchair. He saw what appeared to be a huge hammer on the desk in front of him. He was even more amazed when his grandfather told him to

"Bang that hammer on the bench and say, 'Order in the Court!' really loud!" Sammy looked around, became confused, and said, "Grandpa, I don't see a bench." Judge O'Connell laughed heartily. "That desk in front of you. Bang it on the desk!"

Sammy, delighted at such an instruction, did as he was told. He took the huge hammer in his hand, hit the humongous desk while shouting, "Order! Order! Give me your order!" Sammy then noticed how high above the other chairs he was. He was like a king! He continued, "Order! I want your order!" The only context Sammy had for the word 'order' came from his experience visiting fast food restaurants with his parents. Grandpa objected, "No, no, no! You're not taking orders!" He then thought a moment about how to explain to his grandson that he doesn't work at the drive-thru window. No words immediately came to mind, so he said, "You know what, go ahead. Take your orders."

Sammy continued the great fun: "I want your order! Give me orders! No onions! No pickles! Give me some orders. I love orders!" Thud, thud, thud went Sammy's gavel upon the bench. This was a new and amazing world that his grandpa lived in. Grandpa then gave Sammy an activity book that Wemaw had bought for him. He was set up to fill in the book in the judges' chair while Grandpa worked in his office. Later, Grandpa showed Sammy some strange places in the courtroom: "The witness stand," "the jury box," and "counsel tables." It was like being on a tv show. His brain just couldn't take it all in. Grandpa was delighted to give Sammy a glimpse into his world. He knew it was a lot to take in for an eight-year-old. So, he took Sammy out for an ice cream cone as he explained a little more of what they had seen.

When Sammy arrived home, he burst through the door ready to tell his parents all about the wonders of the Wilson County Courthouse. When he popped through the front door, he immediately noticed tension in the air. Sarah and Phil seemed distant. Sammy found Phil sitting at the kitchen table, and said, “Dad, Grandpa took me to work. I LOVED it! We went inside and there were these huge stairs. I could walk on the giant stairs, or I could take this old-looking elevator. So, you know what I did? I walked up the stairs, and then I took the elevator down! THEN, I took the stairs down and rode the elevator UP! Then Grandpa said, ‘Stop doing that’, so I did. There was nobody there, you know, I wasn’t bothering anyone. After I stopped, he showed me the Room Court!”

“Courtroom,” Phil interjected.

“Right. Hey Dad, what’s wrong?” Sammy noticed that his dad wasn’t really listening to him but had a faraway look in his eyes.

“Oh, sorry son. I was thinking about something else. I’m glad you had a fun time with your grandpa. Let’s talk about it more later, ok?”

“Ok, Dad. I’m going to go outside and play now.”

Phil said, “Great, I may be out there later.”

Just then, Sarah appeared, looking slightly upset. Sammy passed her by on his way outside.

“I’m going outside, Mom.” He noticed her face was flushed. She gave him a quick squeeze of the arm as he passed by.

“Ok, have fun!” she said, trying to sound upbeat.

Sammy grabbed a baseball and glove out of his room before going outside. He opened the front door but felt suddenly drained. He sat down on the front step while setting his glove down beside him. He stared at the baseball in his right hand. “What’s wrong with Mom and Dad?” he thought. “I wish they weren’t sad.”

After passing Sammy, Sarah plopped onto the living

room couch. Phil walked behind her and began rubbing her shoulders. "I'm so sorry, sweetie. I'm disappointed too."

"I know. I really thought I was pregnant this time. Phil, what are we going to do? I don't want Sammy to be in college before he has a sibling. It's been a long road. I'm so tired."

Phil stopped the massage and sat down on the couch next to her. He grabbed her hand while they sat silently for several seconds. He then bowed his head as he prayed softly, "Lord God, what do we do? You see us here, don't You? You know what we've been through trying to conceive another child. It's not working. We are emotionally exhausted. What can we do? What would You have us do? We don't know what to do, but our eyes are on You. Please help! Don't leave us here in this place. We really need You. Please hear our prayer. In Jesus' name. Amen."

Sarah squeezed his hand, "Thank you." After a few seconds, she continued, "I feel better. Any ideas?"

Phil wiped away a tear and smiled. "Yeah! I'm going to go play catch with our boy."

Sarah hugged her husband. "Yes, I love that. Just give me a few minutes. I'll come outside and join you."

Ten minutes later, Sarah breezed out the front door as her son and her husband threw a baseball back and forth to each other across a plush yard of green grass.

She sneakily approached Sammy from behind. Just as he cocked his arm to throw the baseball back to Phil, Sarah attacked. While wrapping her arms around him, she said, "Is this how you tackle someone in baseball? Arggh!!"

On his way down to the ground in his mother's arms, Sammy exclaimed, "Mom!! You don't tackle people in baseball!" They landed in a heap, laughing. Sarah embraced her boy as they remained on the grass. Her grip around him remained tight as he relaxed into her arms. For a moment, he found one of her hands and gave her a pat. Phil plopped down beside them. "Hey Sammy, we need to teach Mom the rules of baseball. I think she has it confused with football." The family laughed together and remained outside most of the evening. They grilled hot dogs, eventually watching the sun go down while playing a card game Sammy had recently learned. Afterward, Sammy went to bed, as his parents talked in their bedroom.

Sarah said to Phil, "Sweetie, thanks for praying earlier. I feel lighter."

Phil smiled back at his wife. "You're welcome."

Sarah continued her thought, "Do you think it's possible the Lord could actually lead us to a solution? And, if he did, could we hear him? And if we could hear Him, would we actually do what He says? Would we trust Him?"

Phil smiled again. "I don't know. Those are good questions."

Sarah stared into the distance. "Yeah."

Phil waited for her gaze to return, now looking her in the eyes. "I'm willing to try. How about you?"

"Yes, let's really try to seek Him." This time, she prayed as they began to drift toward sleep. "Father, I presume You heard all my questions just now. Phil and I … we want to try and seek YOU. We don't know how, but we want to try to hear Your voice. Would You be good to us? Would You be our God? Let us hear from You."

These were the last conscious words said before morning.

5

A REAL NIGHTMARE

Early the next day, Sarah drove from her house to her new place of work at the Poplarton Medical Group. Even though she and Phil had lived in Poplarton for several months now, everything around her childhood hometown still had a new appearance to her eyes. Yet, it was all so familiar. Not all her memories were happy ones. As she made a right turn onto Gordon Avenue, she observed the newly constructed houses that made her stomach momentarily queasy. She then began thinking about Emma.

The remainder of her commute was consumed with thoughts of her childhood best friend. She went back to her first memory of Emma when they met in first grade at Poplarton Elementary. It was a hot day, and Sarah was thirsty when Emma came to her rescue. Sarah recalled standing in front of a vending machine, her palm out with four dimes on it. She thought she had put five in her pocket to purchase a grape soda that day. Mom had said it would be okay if she had just one. But there she stood with forty cents in her hand when she really needed fifty cents. Meanwhile, Emma was looking for someone to play hopscotch with when she found Sarah staring at the vending machine. Sarah replayed this conversation in her mind.

"Want to play hopscotch with me?" asked Emma cheerfully.

"Not really. I want a grape soda, but I lost one of my dimes."

"You lost a dime? That stinks. Let me see if I have a dime." Emma said these words as she began checking all of the pockets of her denim overalls. She put her fingers in her side pockets to discover some lint and a marble. Then she put them in the pouch of the bib to come up empty-handed. Finally, she unzipped a side pocket. Her investigation turned up one silver coin. She turned to Emma with a tinge of disappointment. "I wish I could give you a dime, but all I have is this quarter."

Sarah recalled Emma's retelling of this story to her mother, describing how her eyes got big and how they both squealed with delight. They had recently learned about coins, so something in Sarah knew that a quarter would do the trick. She put her four dimes and Emma's quarter in the vending machine. They got a nice cold grape soda plus two coins back. They were so happy. They shared the soda, and each got a new coin. Sarah was so overjoyed that she insisted that Emma keep the bigger coin.

Their childhood friendship remained close, Sarah now thinking about their high school years. More than anything, Sarah appreciated Emma's faithful friendship and her growing faith in God. Emma was an inspiration to Sarah. Sarah became amazed at Emma's love for God while they were in youth group together. It seemed to Sarah that Emma had a faith that was real and not just talk. Sarah presently recalled the times when she would stress out, and Emma would come to her with a loving look, take her by the hand and pray for her. Sarah noticed that when Emma addressed God, it seemed like He really was her father. Sarah smiled as she drove, thinking about how Emma talked to Him as a beloved child talks to their dad. Emma and her Father had a very sweet relationship. Sarah felt privileged to hear and be included in their conversation from time to time.

As she stopped at the stoplight and waited, Sarah thought about Emma's ability to challenge her to engage, question and think deeply. She now thought of the time when they were sixteen, standing next to each other at a youth retreat. While the youth pastor led a very large group of teens to sing several worship songs together, Emma became bothered. Afterward, while eating a hot dog, Sarah said, "Hey, you seem far away. What's wrong?"

Emma said, "Well, why do we sing ABOUT Jesus? All those songs were about his traits, but I want to sing TO Him. He is present, you know."

Sarah smiled to herself again as she pulled into the parking lot, remembering that Emma often ended sentences like that. She would say, "He is here, you know," or "He isn't dead, you know," or "He loves you, you know." Whenever Emma would say these things, it would irk Sarah to know that while she did know these things, she did not know them as much as Emma seemed to know them. About the worship songs, all Sarah could think to say was, "Oh. Yeah. Ok." Sarah gave the matter much thought, which led to follow-up conversations with Emma and others. As a result, even now, twenty years later, Sarah realized that she prefers hymns and worship songs that presume Jesus is in the room. She concluded that it IS better to sing to Him rather than about Him.

As Sarah now walked from her car toward the staff entrance, she felt a pang of disappointment about losing touch with Emma. After high school graduation, Sarah and Emma pursued college degrees in different parts of the state.

Even though they attended different colleges, they still talked on the phone semi-regularly. Further, they always saw each other during the holidays as much as they could. After college, Emma married Frank, and Sarah went to medical school. Although they were no longer close, Sarah still felt the influence of Emma's living faith with the survival of her own faith through several years of medical training and residency.

Sarah had not thought of her friend in quite some time, but it made her sad that such fond feelings were triggered by the new houses of the Holbrook neighborhood. Sarah hated those new houses for good reason. Throughout that day in the clinic, Sarah noticed she was seeing an abnormally high number of patients from the Holbrook neighborhood. She thought of her dear friend and wished she were there to pray with her now.

She arrived home in the evening as Phil was making dinner. After a quick greeting and a shower, Sarah arrived at the dinner table.

While passing potatoes, Phil said, "So, how was your day?" Sarah passed the salad to Sammy. "Actually, it was strange. Today had a weird vibe."

Phil said, "Oh?"

"I thought a lot about Emma today. It's been a while, you know? I haven't thought of her in quite a while. Of course, I always pass by that Holbrook neighborhood on my way to work."

Phil grimaced. "Maybe you should change your route."

"Yeah, and then I had several patients from Holbrook. It creeped me out a little. Weird day."

Phil raised an eyebrow while blowing on his food-filled fork. "I'm glad you're home now. Aren't you, Sammy?"

Sammy quickly replied, "Yeah!" as Phil continued speaking. "I'm glad you thought of Emma, though. I'm still so thankful for her."

Sammy questioned, "Who's Emma?"

"She was my best friend in school. She's very dear to me, and I miss her."

"Oh! Maybe you should go see her! She sounds nice."

Phil and Sarah glanced at each other. After a moment's pause, Sarah said, "Yeah. I'd like to. I'd love to see her again."

The Marshall family of three entered their bedtime routines after dinner and went to sleep. Suddenly, Sarah's ears filled with the shrill sound of a tornado siren. She tried to rush over to the window and look outside, but her feet were stuck. She could hardly move at all. Emma suddenly appeared before her. "Emma!" she said. "I've been thinking of you all day!" She didn't respond to Sarah, as Sarah realized she was no longer at home. She had been transported to the Ortega's house. Sarah watched Emma as she rushed around her house trying to wake everyone up. "Frank, get up, there's a tornado!" she said. Sarah watched Emma as she scrambled down the hall into her son's room. "Manny, wake up, sweetie. We need to get into the bathroom. Oh! Let's grab your pillow. C'mon sweetie. Quickly, now!"

Sarah could now see the Ortega family of three gathered in the bathroom. Frank grabbed Manny's mattress. He placed it over Manny in the bathtub. Sarah's heart pounded as she felt the tornado approach. In a state of panic, she screamed, "Run! Run away! Get away from it! Oh God, not again!!!"

Sarah jolted awake as Phil's hand squeezed her arm. He said, "Hey, hey, wake up. You're having a nightmare." Sarah could feel her heart racing and adrenaline pumping. There was sweat down her neck and tears in her eyes. She said, "Oh God!" Phil said, "Hey, you're ok. It was a bad dream. I'm here." Holding her now: "I've got you. I've got you. You're ok. Shhh, you're ok. I'm so sorry."

She cried into his shoulder. It was 3:45 am. She whispered, "It was a tornado. It was Emma."

Phil squeezed her tightly. "Do you want to talk about it?"

Slightly louder, she said, "No. Just hold me like this. Don't let me go back to sleep."

After a few seconds, Phil replied, "I can do that."

6

A HARDENED DREAMER

There weren't many options available for Sarah's commute that didn't involve driving by the Holbrook addition. "That's okay," she thought. She was in a defiant mood that morning and didn't waver from her normal routine. After making the customary right turn onto Gordon Avenue, she stared at the new homes built after the previous neighborhood was destroyed. An EF-5 tornado demolished everything in its wake on May 9th, 2017. Most of the houses on the northwest side of Poplarton were turned to rubble. Sarah was awoken that night by her parents calling to let her know they were ok. The storm had passed one mile north of them. Her dad would call her back later that afternoon to tell her that her friend Emma did not make it through the night. Neither did Frank. Even though that phone call had come eight years prior, if Sarah lingered over the memory, it would still bring forth tears.

A few hours after Sarah arrived at work, Nancy, a staff nurse, approached Sarah. She said, "Dr. Marshall, are you ok today? You seem a little distant… not quite yourself."

"I know. I'm struggling to summon compassion for my

patients. You're right. That's not like me. Actually, I'm struggling emotionally. I had a terrible dream last night that kept me up afterward. It was one of those dreams that seemed very real and involved loved ones. I'm kind of a mess." Sarah took a deep breath. "Nancy, could you pray for me to make it through my rounds? Ugh. I'm gutting it out."

"Yes, of course. Is there anything more I can do?"

"I don't know. I'm constantly fighting the urge to coil into a ball and whimper, but I can't do that, can I? So, I've gone numb instead."

"I see. Hang in there. We're here to support you. You know that."

"Thank you." She drew another deep breath. She walked towards the nearby exam room, picked up the patient file. "Ok, who's next?"

Phil watched intently that evening for his wife's arrival home. He went out to greet her with a warm embrace. After a few moments, Sarah stepped back, placed both hands on Phil's shoulders, and squeezed. "I need a moment," she said. "I think I may go for a walk."

"Sure, can I help?"

"I don't know. I'm really upset with God."

"About the dream?"

"Well yeah, the dream was terrifying. I mean, I know it's been eight years, but it is like I lived through the tornado and they didn't. Plus, you and I, we sincerely sought Him the night before about what we do next, right?"

"Right."

"Well, I feel like ever since we prayed together, I've had constant reminders of suffering and trauma. I drive daily by the neighborhood I can't seem to avoid. I have had numerous patients from Holbrook. Now I'm suffering from lack of sleep due to a horrific dream. I'm overwhelmed, and discouraged. I don't feel like He cares for us." She looked deep into her husband's eyes through fresh tears.

Gazing back, he said, "Let's go inside and tell Him how you feel. I'll pray with you, but you should be honest with Him. I'm frustrated too, but let's not turn back now. Ok?"

"Phil, I'm exhausted but… ok."

After following her husband inside to their bedroom, she shut the door. Sitting down, Phil took his wife's hand. He prayed calmly. "Father, we come confused and frustrated."

Sarah interrupted.

"Who do You think You are? We came to You for help, and You treat us like THIS?"

Phil smiled to himself, "Yes… go ahead and tell Him."

She continued, "I thought You cared for us! Instead, You remind me of my dear friend… then terrify me with a dream of Your destruction? What kind of God are You? How can there be any redemption in this story? It's so very, very painful. You must know that."

A few seconds passed, and she continued further:

"Look, I'm an emotional mess. I can't get pregnant, and when I come to You for help, I get this nonsense! I don't need Your show of power right now. Just, You know what I need? I need You to be a good dad. Be a good dad. Love me. Why give me a stone when I ask for bread? I can't see the connection. Connect the dots for us. Please. Be a good dad."

Sarah saw Phil give a half-grin as they came out of the bedroom.

"I'm sorry if I was a little loud and irreverent," she said.

"Did you get it all off your chest?"

"Yes. Sometimes I'm surprised He doesn't strike me down."

"I'm actually amazed at your relationship with God. I love how open you are with Him. You never hide your feelings. I bet He loves that about you."

Sammy appeared from his room as he heard his mom say, “He puts up with me.”

MEANWHILE, on the other side of Poplarton, Manny was about to have a dream of his own.

He had not spoken to Lucas for several months, but as Manny walked down the long, dark hallway on his way to the bathroom in the middle of the night, Lucas was waiting.

He came out of a dark corner and said, “Hey, loser, I hear you’ve been talking about me.”

Manny gave a startled reply, “Stay away from me, Lucas.”

“Oh, I’m not going anywhere. You know what? You’re not either. You’re twelve now. Twelve-year-olds don’t get adopted. You know that, right? Besides, who would adopt you? No, dude, you and I are here for the long haul. I’m not going away.”

Manny stood in a defensive posture and said, “Get out of my way. I don’t have to listen to you.”

Lucas took a step toward him. “You better listen to me. I’m the only friend you’ve got in here. Nobody likes you. You’re dumb and ugly. Other kids only talk to you because they feel sorry for you.”

Just then, a door opened, and they saw a flashlight. The paid security officer came down the hall. He whispered loudly, “Hey, what’s going on in here? We need to keep this hall clear!”

Lucas answered, “Oh! Sorry sir. This kid was teasing me and calling me names.”

The security officer fired back, “You’re the victim, Lucas? I’m not an idiot. Go back to bed. Both of you!”

They walked back down the hall together toward their separate rooms. The security officer went back to his post, closing the door at the end of the hallway. Lucas shoved Manny, but Manny kept walking, walked into his room, and closed the door behind him.

Manny was content to escape the encounter with Lucas and fell asleep quickly. As he slept, he began to dream. Suddenly, he was standing in court before Judge O'Connell. Judge O'Connell then stood up and pointed his finger at Manny, saying, "You're guilty! GUILTY! You ARE a thief! You ARE a loser. You ARE dumb! You ARE ugly! NOBODY likes you!" With each proclamation, a lightning bolt flew out of Judge Frankenstein's scar toward Manny. Each time, Manny would duck or hide behind the table and each time the lightning bolt would narrowly miss Manny's head. Dissatisfied with the imprecise lightning strikes, the robed figure then whipped up a large wind, sending the swirling twister in Manny's direction. Manny tried to run from it, but his feet were stuck. He felt his hair start to blow, but awoke suddenly. He was gasping for air and sweating. One of his three roommates shouted at him. "Shut up, Manny! You woke me up, stupid!"

"Sorry, I just... I... I had a bad dream."

"I'm not your mommy. Shut it!"

Manny was seated up in bed, but then collapsed back onto his pillow. The twelve-year-old tried to be quiet. He tried not to cry. Mercifully, the other roommates all went back to sleep and never heard the sniffles coming from Manny's despair. He thought to himself, "I'm such a baby! I'm too soft. I must get harder. I must get tougher. I must get meaner."

As Mr. Phipps was walking through the dining hall the next morning, he stopped at Manny's table. Mr. Phipps told Manny that he wanted to speak with him. "Can you come by my office at 9 am?"

Manny said, "Yes, sir!" as Mr. Phipps walked away.

Manny presumed that Mr. Phipps wanted to speak with him about his encounter with Lucas the night before. "Surely, security didn't actually BELIEVE Lucas!" he thought. The other kids at the table made the customary remarks like "You're in trouble!" and "He's going to tear you up!" Manny was actually pleased at their reaction because it might help his reputation. His personal vow to toughen up was already paying off.

At 9 AM, Mr. Phipps invited Manny into his office and said, "I want to talk to you about something that might help you, Manny. I'm starting a little Bible study here in my office for the older boys. Well, some of the older boys. Actually, I'm only inviting a few to join me. We will meet every Saturday morning at 8 AM. I won't expect a lot out of you, but I will expect you to read what's assigned. That's all. What do you say?"

"God? You want to talk to me about God? Mr. Phipps, God hates me! You understand that He killed my parents, right? He tried to kill me, but missed. He'll kill me someday, I imagine. Besides, I'm a thief! Thieves don't attend Bible studies." Manny felt good about this response. It was tough and, as he saw it, it was true.

"I'm sorry you feel that way. I think you're wrong about Him. I don't think He hates you. I think He loves you."

Manny angrily replied, "Mr. Phipps, don't waste your time. You're a nice man, but you'll never convince me God isn't out to get me. I'm sorry, but your Bible study isn't for me."

"I see. I pray someday you will see Him differently. I pray one day you will see love in His eyes when He looks at you."

"Ok, you do that. Can I go now?"

It was Saturday, and the Marshalls were on a walk in a local park. Sammy was up ahead of Phil and Sarah, exploring the trail up ahead. While walking along the gravel path, Phil said to Sarah, "Hey, I did something last night. I searched for the old news story on the tornado, and there was mention of the Ortegas."

"Ha, that's interesting. I did the same thing!"

Phil said, "Did you see what it said about their son?"

"Yeah, he was found roaming about the rubble."

Just then, Sammy called out to Phil, who rushed ahead. After commenting on the strange rock Sammy had found, Phil went back by Sarah's side. He said, "Yeesh, a four-year-old roaming about the rubble looking for his parents. How sad is that?"

"I know. I don't think I want to talk about it anymore."

After walking the next fifty yards in silence, Sarah said, "I heard he went to live with her sister."

"Who?"

He then realized who she meant. "Oh, really? The boy, you mean?"

"Yes. But then my parents later told me that she became ill or something happened where she couldn't take care of him."

"What happened to him?"

"I'm not sure. He most likely wound up with another relative."

Just then, Sammy discovered a small snake and called them over to take a look.

After commenting on the snake's stripe and coloring, the couple was alone again as Sammy ran up ahead.

While standing under a large live oak tree, Sarah said to Phil. "Do you think it's strange that we independently read the same news article last night?"

"Yeah, one from 2017. I guess I was a little affected by your dream as well. I'm sorry. Is that weird to you?"

"No, no, it's fine," she said. "You're entitled to be curious."

After some sips from a water bottle, Sarah said, "Do you think it means anything? Or just a coincidence? Remember, we said we would try."

"Try what?" But he then recovered himself once again. "Oh right! Yes, listening to the Lord. Wait, are you suggesting we…?"

Interrupting Sarah said, "I don't know. I just wonder if maybe we should find out what happened to him?"

"The boy?" Phil said.

"Yeah, his name is Emmanuel. It's spelled with two M's. I remember because it has 'Emma' at the front."

"That's cool. I like that."

Sammy then approached his parents to tell them he was tired and ready to go home. The family of three hiked back to the car, never mentioning Emmanuel Ortega again that day.

7

SEARCHING

On the following Saturday, Sarah greeted her parents as she breezed through their front door entryway. Wemaw spoke first. "Good morning, dear. It's so nice to get time with you this morning, but we'll miss your boys."

"Thanks, Mom. Phil called me a few minutes ago. Sammy is having the time of his life on the campout." Sarah entered the kitchen and was met by the smell of sausage, eggs, and biscuits.

"Breakfast smells great. You didn't have to cook for me."

"We were happy to, and I was hungry," Grandpa said with a smile. "I forget. Was it a Boy Scout campout?"

"Cub Scouts."

"Ah, yes. They will come back with stories."

After the meal and pleasant conversation, Wemaw excused herself to take a phone call from a dear friend. Sarah remained at the table with Grandpa. "Hey Dad, I'd like to ask you about something."

"Shoot!"

"Well, with all of your law enforcement contacts and,

well, you know, all the people you know in the county, would you mind checking into something? It's a bit of a mystery."

He gobbled up a leftover sausage link and said, "Hmm, sounds intriguing. What is it?"

"I've been thinking a lot about Emma lately."

"Oh, Sweetie," said Wemaw with a wince as she sat back down at the table.

"Dad, is there any way to find out if her son is okay or where he might be? I'd just like to know that he is ok."

Grandpa took a sip of his coffee. "Well, I don't know. I can try. It's been several years, sweetheart. I don't know where I would begin. What's his name?"

"Emmanuel Ortega. With two M's at the front. You know, 'Emma'. It's unusual."

"Emmanuel with two M's, you say?" he responded with a raised eyebrow.

"Yeah."

Deep in thought now, he said, "Wait just a minute. I need to write that down." After pulling out his pen and writing the name on a napkin, he said, "You know, dear, I may not need to consult with anyone. Give me some time to consult my notes, ok? It's been several months, but I seem to recall seeing that name on some court documents. How old is he, like eleven or twelve?"

"Oh no, is he in some kind of trouble? I mean, yeah, he was four in 2017, so yeah, that would make him twelve now."

"I can't go into detail about the court stuff, you know that. But, let me check my old dockets, and see if there's anything I can share about him if that was really him at teen court."

"That's amazing, Dad. Thank you!"

"Of course," said he.

When her boys returned later that day, Sarah told Phil about her conversation with her dad. Sammy overheard and said, "Hey mom, I'm glad Grandpa can help you! Who's Emmanuel?"

"Do you remember when I was talking about my friend Emma the other day? Emmanuel is Emma's son."

"Oh! Is he eight like me?"

"A few years older than you. Like, twelve."

Impressed, Sammy said, "Twelve. He's really old. Much bigger than me. I've been arm wrestling boys at school, Mom. This kid would probably beat me at arm wrestling."

Phil interrupted and said, "Sammy, I'll show you a few tricks. Let's arm wrestle after dinner."

"With you, Dad? Yes! Wait, you'll beat me for sure! What can I do?"

"I'll show you."

Sammy excitedly replied, "Oh yeah!"

That afternoon, Grandpa went to the office so he could start looking through the past teen court dockets. He looked in January but found nothing. The February docket was missing, but as he thumbed through the names from March, he found a file. "Emmanuel Ortega."

He fondly recalled the boy now. He was with Mr. Phipps from the boys' home. "Ha, I think I may have prayed for that boy! Amazing!" thought Grandpa. "I've got to tell Sarah."

A few minutes later, Sarah answered the phone.

"Sweetie, I can't go into detail, but I suggest you call Henry Phipps at the boys' home for information on Emmanuel."

"He lives at the orphanage?" asked Sarah.

"Call Mr. Phipps."

"Dad, no one's taken care of him all these years. That's so sad."

"Sarah, I've actually prayed for this boy. I remember him."

"That's wonderful! I believe you. You may have the

opportunity to pray for him again." After a few seconds of silence, she said, "I'll call Mr. Phipps."

After hanging up with her dad, she found Phil in their bedroom. "What was that about?" said Phil. "That was my dad," she said. "Phil, do you remember my prayer in here a few days ago?"

"Yeah! You were mad."

"Yeah, I feel kinda bad about that," said Sarah. "Actually, the Lord seems to be answering that prayer as only He can."

"Really?"

"Yeah, I asked Dad about Emmanuel at breakfast this morning. I told you that. Well, Dad just said that he knows him. Phil—he's actually prayed for him. AND, he knows where he lives!"

"So where does he live?"

Sarah grimaced. "The boys' home."

"He's still an orphan?"

"Yeah, he's still an orphan. Dad said I could call Mr. Phipps at the orphanage for further information. Phil, I think we should call about him."

"Whoa, whoa! Sarah, hold on. When you say 'call about him', what do you mean?"

"I mean call. Ask questions. I don't know. Maybe meet him?"

Phil lowered his tone. "Meet him? We don't know anything about this kid. He's a twelve-year-old orphan who has been in the system most of his life. If your dad knows him, he's probably been in some trouble. He may be a bad kid for all we know."

"That's why we would meet him. That's how we find out. What's the harm?"

"You could fall in love with him and then have your heart broken. That's the potential harm."

"Take it up with the Lord, Phil! Don't you see? He's

connecting the dots. He's trying to lead us. Will we trust Him? Will we do what He says?"

Phil said, "Ok, ok. It's just going really fast. Let's take it one step at a time. Let's call this Mr. Phelps."

She interrupted. "Phipps."

He continued, "Let's call the guy and see what we can find out."

On Monday at 9:07 AM, Mr. Phipps smiled as he heard the lady on the phone express her desire for information.

"Yes ma'am, Mrs. Marshall, is it? Yes, Mrs. Marshall, we typically like to do this sort of thing in person. I'm happy to make an appointment with you if you'd like to come to my office and visit. I don't like to give out information about the boys over the phone, you see."

He then responded to her next question, "Oh yes, Manny does live here. I can tell you that much."

He then responded again, "Oh yes, next Saturday would be fine. 9 AM? Yes, see you then."

After the call, Mr. Phipps said, "Mrs. Spinorkle, please mark my calendar for next Saturday at 9. I'm meeting with a Mrs. Marshall about Manny."

These types of meetings were never intentionally divulged to the orphan ahead of time. This policy was followed to prevent inflated hopes and expectations for the child. However, whether it was by Mrs. Spinorkle's indiscretion or the wandering eyes of other office staff, the news always spread among the boys' home population that there was interest in a kid.

Unfortunately, the first kid to receive this whispered news was Lucas. He became immediately enraged with unbridled jealousy. His hurt feelings immediately went to work. "I won't let this happen," he thought. There was too much at stake. Orphan life had certain laws which must be maintained. *Lucas law number one* was that no child older than ten years of age could ever be adopted. Never ever. *Lucas law number two* established a pecking order. Since Lucas was the oldest boy at age fifteen, what he says goes. Not more than two weeks earlier, he told Manny that there was no way he would ever leave the orphanage. Lucas was a law unto himself, so his word was final. No exceptions. Such was the logic in his mind.

His first objective was to keep the news of this meeting from reaching Manny. By use of threatened force and intimidation, he shut down the rumor mill immediately. Next, his brain hatched a plan that involved two elements. The first was a pocketknife. The second was pain.

8

APPOINTMENTS

The anticipation and momentum toward Saturday were building in Sarah's heart. On Wednesday, she said to Phil, "Do you think we should take Sammy? I think maybe we should take Sammy." Phil looked at her, then looked toward the window. Sarah continued, "It's just that Mr. Phipps said we could possibly meet Emmanuel on Saturday. At the very least, I wonder if we should let Sammy know what's going on."

Phil thought a moment and then looked at his wife. "I think I need you to tell me what's going on. Dear, we can't just go and pick out a child like you pick out a puppy at the pound. I knew this would happen. In your heart, you have jumped to step number nine when we haven't started step number one. Sarah, sweetie, I'm already concerned about seeing your hopes and dreams dashed by this kid. Can you imagine what it might do to Sammy if we give him hope of a brother before such hope is warranted? Let's not do that to him. You and I are meeting with Mr. Phipps on Saturday. Let's keep it that way. No, let's not involve Sammy. Not now."

"I know. You're right. I jumped ahead. I do that. I know

we aren't picking out a pound puppy, though. My excitement is at least partially generated by this. We sought God. I sense that He is at work. I sense He is moving. I believe He is good. Don't you? When we meet with Mr. Phipps, I expect the Lord to meet us there too."

"Fair enough. I agree that He has taken us to this step. Let's take it with Him and not get ahead of Him. Let's see what He does."

The couple held hands and prayed together once more.

On Thursday, Manny still knew nothing of Mr. Phipps' upcoming meeting. Weeks earlier, Manny had determined that orphanage survival hinged on a tougher image. Therefore, he decided to stop avoiding Lucas. "When he looks at me, I'll look right back", he thought. "And if something happens between us, nothing could help me more than to beat him up. I'm done with being afraid of him."

That afternoon, Manny looked across the dining hall, and there was Lucas. They locked eyes. Neither would withdraw their gaze. Lucas said, "You gotta problem Ortega?"

Manny replied, "Yeah. You."

"Yeah, I'm your problem all right. Let's settle this."

"Outside? On the playground? The parking lot? Anywhere Lucas! Any time."

Lucas, wanting to get Manny alone, said, "Tomorrow. 10 am behind the gym. Just you and me. Nobody else."

"I'll be there."

Lucas spent Thursday night sharpening his knife. He wanted the blade smooth, so it didn't tear flesh on its way in or out. Lucas knew that if he beat up Manny or stabbed him, it wouldn't damage his opportunity at adoption. Instead, now that the fight challenge was public, Lucas planned to stab himself in the arm. If he then blamed Manny for the wound on his trip to the Emergency Room, then the police investigation would ensure that no one would want Manny.

Manny couldn't fall asleep that night in anticipation. He actually wasn't afraid. He was ready. It was time for him to be hardened. It was time for him to grow up. Beat up or be beaten up. Sure, Lucas was older, but Manny was slightly bigger. "After tomorrow, the boys will look at me differently", he thought. "They will respect me, or they will bury me." Either way, Manny contented himself as he eventually slept soundly that night.

At 9:45 am, Manny was pacing around campus. At 9:50, he was behind the building waiting for Lucas. At precisely 9:53 am, Manny felt a hard tug on his shirt from behind. He heard a gruff voice say, "You're coming with me, you idiot." Had he been ambushed? "Of course! That cheat Lucas wanted me alone, so he could tag-team me with one of his henchmen. Who is it? Toby? He's dragging me away!" All these thoughts entered Manny's mind as he tried to ascertain his captor. It wasn't Toby. It was Henry.

Henry Phipps had such an intense grip on Manny's shirt collar and pulled him toward his car. He opened the back seat and threw him in. "You're coming with me! You're staying at my house tonight. I'm not going to let you blow this. How can you be so stupid?" said Mr. Phipps.

Manny was suddenly dumbfounded by these events. "Mr. Phipps? Why? What are you doing?" Getting no reply from Mr. Phipps as he drove, Manny continued, "Why are you saying I'm stupid? Blow what?"

Mr. Phipps, now stopped at a stoplight, turned his head around. "There's a family coming to meet with me tomorrow. About you. They want to talk to me about you. You get it?"

Manny sat in the back seat silently. Five minutes ago, he was preparing to fight Lucas. Now, he's in the back of a car headed for a safe haven. Mr. Phipps, still frustrated, uttered in a hushed tone, but still loud enough to hear, "I'm trying to save you from yourself."

Manny, still trying to understand, said, "A family is interested in me?"

"Yes, as hard as that is for me to believe right now, that is the truth. 9 am tomorrow. Until then, I'm not letting you out of my sight."

Manny never dared to ask, and he never found out how Mr. Phipps knew about his scheduled fight with Lucas. Manny never knew that Lucas was waiting to stab himself and blame Manny. Manny never knew many things, but he would eventually know the One who fights for him in ways that are both known and unknown.

9

LOVE APPEARS

It was 12:30 pm on Saturday and Mr. Phipps was headed home after his meeting with Mr. and Mrs. Marshall. He had a twinkle in his eye along with a spring in his step as he exited his vehicle. He walked down his driveway toward the front door. Manny wasn't with him this time. He was told to stay at the boys' home to wait further instruction.

As Mr. Phipps entered his front door and walked toward the dining room, he saw his dear wife. She said, "You're back! Great. Let's have some lunch." Henry Phipps said to his beloved, "Yes, that sounds wonderful. Jackie, I want to thank you again for helping me host the boy last night. I just saw no way around it. I know that was unusual. I'll try not to make it a habit."

Jaqueline Phipps responded to her husband, "Dear, I didn't mind. Besides, the boy was sweet. No bother. What happened with him and the couple today?"

"It was rather remarkable. I sat them down, noting that they were a lovely couple: Mr. and Mrs. Marshall. I noticed they were holding hands. Anyway, as I talked about the boy and told them about his background, the lady stared at me blankly. She gave me very little emotional response. Actually, this boy has quite a poignant family history. His parents were killed in the tornado."

Mrs. Phipps exclaimed sympathetically, "Oh Henry."

He continued, "I know, but it was as if the lady knew all about it. The man didn't really look at me. He watched his wife. They would nod politely, but I thought to myself, 'This is going nowhere.' I offered them tea and refreshment, but they took none. After I talked about the boys' home policies and procedures, I concluded by asking if they wanted to meet Manny. I somewhat expected them to decline, but the man looked at his wife. She smiled and said to me, 'That is what we are here to do.' As soon as Manny entered the room, the lady approached him and embraced him. The boy was quite taken aback by this..."

Mrs. Phipps interjected, "I'm sure he was! Oh, dear. We have those leftovers from last night. How about I heat them up for lunch?"

"Oh, that will be fine. Anyway, she hugged the life out of him saying, 'Emmanuel, I know you. I knew your mother. I can see her in your face and in your name. She was my best friend when we were kids, and I loved her.'"

"How remarkable!" said Mrs. Phipps while scrounging through the refrigerator.

"Yeah! And THEN she said, 'Emmanuel, she (referring to his mother) had such faith in God.' Here is where I interrupted and said, 'He goes by Manny.' But she said, 'We'll see about that.'"

Mrs. Phipps laughed. "Wow."

Jackie's husband continued, "Yeah. Anyway, she went on to tell the boy that God wanted her and her husband to come and meet him. She kept insisting that they were there on God's errand. She said that someday she would tell him about how they just knew it was God that sent them to this meeting. Jackie, this lady looked the boy directly in the face and said, 'Emmanuel, more than anything, I just want you to know you are loved. God is good, and He loves you. Your lovely mother would want you to know that you are precious to God. Ok? You are precious to Him.'"

"What did he say? The boy. What did the boy say?"

"Ha, what could he say? He stood there and received her blessing. He was dumbfounded. But, you know, dear, there is something else. A few weeks ago, I invited Manny to the young men's Bible study. In response, he told me that God hated him and was surely out to get him."

"Of course. His family was consumed by a tornado."

"I know. But I told him I would pray that his concept of God would change, uhm, that he would find out that God loves him. Ha, he practically dared me to pray that prayer. So, I did. It amazed me when this stranger showed up today to tell him that his mother wanted him to know that he is precious to God. Well, how great is that?"

"Pretty great," she said. She then continued, "Well, do you think it's going anywhere in terms of adoption?"

"That, I don't know. The next step would be a supervised home visit. We shall see if they want to schedule that. I'd be happy to take Manny over to their house, though. They seem like good people."

Manny's reaction to the meeting with Sarah and Phil Marshall was bewilderment. He walked into the meeting as a certain person. But, his person and his ideas about the real world were seemingly hugged out of him by a strange lady. How could everything change with a single hug? Manny knew deep down, though, that it was no ordinary hug. He was hugged intensely by an angel lady who came with a message from his mother. He said out loud to himself, "Is that really what happened?"

He couldn't stop thinking about Sarah. He thought, "Why was she looking at me that way? Why did I seem to mean so much to her?" In his mind, he could look at her looking at him. She had a beautiful radiance and internal light. Was she even real? He could only categorize her as an angel lady, because that was the only word he knew for divinity in human form.

So Manny wrestled with this divine hug and what it could mean for his future. Then he heard a voice inside that said, "You must not get carried away. You're still an orphan. You still live in an orphanage. You still have to survive in here. Nothing has changed. You're still the same."

The Marshalls also felt the aftershocks of the meeting. Phil and Sarah had arranged for Sammy to spend the day with his grandparents, so they could meet Mr. Phipps and then have time afterward to process together over lunch.

"Sarah, you really came alive in there. Were you intending such an impassioned speech?"

"No, I wasn't. When I saw him, I was moved. All of a sudden, I felt such compassion. It seemed to come out of this well inside me. I surprised myself, but it was wonderful. I'm actually exhausted now. Will you pass those onion rings? Do you think I shocked him? Scared him?"

"Yes, you shocked him, but you didn't scare him, I don't think," Phil said with a smile. He continued. "Sarah, something happened to me in there also. I've been pretty cautious about today's meeting. You know that. But, well, I don't know if it's all the praying we've been doing, but I think we should get to know him more. Whatever the next step is, I think we need to take it."

"Oh, really?"

"Yes, I know you're surprised because I was unsure before..."

"No, it's not that," she interrupted. "At this very moment, I feel like I've done what I was supposed to do. Obviously, I didn't know that I would passionately proclaim a message of love from his mother, but now that I've done that, I feel fulfilled. Like, maybe that was it?"

"Yes, but the reaction in my heart to your impassioned words was that there must be more than words. And more than a single hug. I felt love for the kid, too. There's something in me that wants to show love to the kid."

Sarah said, "I'm glad you feel that way." Then something seemed to seize Sarah's heart, and she exclaimed, "Oh! Phil, I forgot to do something. I really, really wanted him to know that my dad had prayed for him. Oh, I blew it!"

"Hey, don't beat yourself up. Emmanuel doesn't know your dad. Not yet. You can tell him another time, or maybe Grandpa can tell him himself someday."

"Yes. Ok. That makes me feel better. They have met though, you know. Evidently, Emmanuel was on Dad's teen court docket once."

"That's right. I forgot you had shared that with me. Well, I doubt the kid remembers him."

In a low voice that trailed off, Sarah said, "Yeah. Probably not."

"All things have been committed to me by my Father. No one knows the Son except the Father, and no one knows the Father except the Son and those to whom the Son chooses to reveal him.

Matthew 11:27

10

ONE STEP FORWARD, ONE STEP OUT THE DOOR

On the morning of the home visit, Manny woke up with confused and complex emotions. His heart was seized with the unfamiliar feeling of hope mixed with the quite familiar feeling of suspicion and disbelief that anything good could happen to him. While he brushed his teeth, one of his dorm roommates approached him with a raised eyebrow and a mocking voice:

"Hey roomie, how do you feel about dinner tonight? Try not to blow it. I like the idea of one less kid in this room."

Manny took a moment searching for words to describe his feelings. Finding none, he shrugged his shoulders, "Good, I guess. I mean, whatever."

The truth was that this was a very significant event for Manny. Many years later he reflected on this precise moment of personal history, pouring out his feelings in a journal entry:

"In my youth, I was a wall builder. Throughout my early years, brick by brick and stone by stone, I

constructed a sturdy and magnificent wall around myself. My wall was high. It was thick. It was strong. The wall of self-protection had become so familiar to me that I didn't consciously know it was there. But it was. The strong wall surrounded me and became my home.

As I think of it now, I can visualize it. The wall's foundation consisted of a long-held belief. I had been told from an early age that it was an "act of God" that had destroyed my parents. On May 6, 2017, I escaped God's wrath but surely God would come for me again. Surely, He would get me eventually. I really believed that. Yikes. Upon such a foundation, I constructed my wall with the building blocks of fear and misunderstanding. Whatever God did to pursue me, I interpreted through the foundational lens of God-fright and suspicion. Therefore, every act of kindness and love from God, I misinterpreted as hate. Each of these misunderstandings resulted in another brick in the wall. God's smile toward me was constantly turned upside down. Every offered loaf of bread I received as if it were a stone... another stone in my edifice of self-defense.

Mr. Phipps' proclamation of God's love toward me produced only a slight breeze against my wall, but Sarah's hug was a full-scale assault upon it. Afterward, I was uneasy and undone. Life no longer made sense to me. It made less sense when Mr. Phipps came to me and told me that the nice lady and man *wanted to have me over for dinner. Mr. Phipps joined us in order to determine whether it was a proper home for adoption. As I considered what this dinner could mean for my life, I started to experience the unfamiliar feeling of hope. But then again, I desperately did not want to be tricked, so I had to keep my guard up. After all, Lucas had told me that no kid my age ever gets adopted. So I decided to view the upcoming home visit with a suspicious eye."*

Mr. Phipps pulled up to the curb in front of the Marshall house. Manny took a deep breath as he walked behind Mr. Phipps toward the door. As they approached the doorbell, the front door flung open. A blur of an image ran toward Manny. Manny suddenly felt an embrace around his midsection. He looked down, and there was Sammy. Without thinking, he said, "Hey, kid!" Sammy let go, looked up into Manny's face, saying, "Oh, sorry, I'm Sammy! Do you want to arm wrestle?" Before Manny could respond, he felt himself dragged into the house by the strange boy. Mr. Phipps smiled while greeting Sarah and Phil, who were standing at the front door, expressing shock at their son's greeting.

Their shock intensified several seconds later when they heard Manny's muffled scream from somewhere in the house behind them. Sarah, Phil, and Mr. Phipps rushed into the living room to find Manny had tackled Sammy, but they were then laughing. Phil said, "What happened? Are you ok Manny?"

"Yeah," he said, smiling. "This kid wanted me to arm

wrestle him, so I did. I was just about to pin his arm to the table when… when… he licked my hand!"

Sammy, laughing, said, "You taught me that move, Dad!"

Sarah and Phil, now with anguished expression, heard Manny say further, "He's a cheater! I was so surprised, that the kid pinned my hand down and won." At this, Sammy approached Phil with an extended open palm, expecting his dad to give him a high five.

Phil swiped Sammy's hand down as Sarah exclaimed, "Sammy! Manny, I'm sorry dear. Mr. Phipps, I'm afraid we aren't off to a good start. Our son was just so excited to meet Manny…"

A FEW WEEKS LATER, Sarah related these events to Judge O'Connell while visiting her parents at home. "Dad, I wanted to laugh and cry at the same time. You should have seen Mr. Phipps' face. I'm surprised he didn't march Manny right out of our house at that point."

Grandpa smiled broadly. "That's my number one grandson! In a funny way, it sounds like the perfect beginning. At least the boy felt wanted. Did it calm down after that?"

"Yes, over dinner I described Manny's mom to him in greater detail. I described our friendship and how influential she was on my life and my faith. He was quiet, but I'm sure he liked hearing more about her."

Grandpa nodded. "Of course."

"By the way, where's Mom?"

"Oh! She's painting at a friend's house. Mrs. Buckley. She's with her."

Sarah nodded, smiled, and continued, "Oh! And I overheard a sweet little conversation after dinner. Sammy told

Manny what a great grandpa he had. I mean, you know, a grandpa that's great."

"Yes, I get your meaning. That's wonderful. That boy is a treasure to me."

"Anyway, Mr. Phipps has been great. We actually have a court date now. Can you believe it Dad? Manny will officially join our family on June 8th! Amazing!"

"Sarah, you know how I feel about adoption hearings. They are my absolute favorite thing to preside over. It will be a precious event. I'm so sorry we will miss it."

"Don't worry Dad. I know you and Mom planned your trip to Ireland long ago. The timing just can't be helped. Besides, Manny can meet his new grandparents when you get back. I'm sure he will love you. I know you and Mom will love him."

Grandpa reflected a moment and replied, "I just can't believe that the boy I once prayed for in my office will soon be my new grandson. What a blessing."

The following weeks were special for Manny. As the official adoption date approached, Phil and Sammy would often pick him up from the boys' home and go for ice cream or mini-golf or a movie. On occasion, Sarah would pick him up, bringing him home for dinner or a play date with Sammy. Mr. Phipps would accompany them from time to time. He made his reports, but Mr. Phipps was convinced from the first meeting that the Marshalls were a fit household for adoption. Somehow, Mr. Phipps ensured that Lucas and his friends were kept away from Manny, so he was able to live peacefully until the day he moved out.

Three weeks prior to the scheduled adoption hearing, Mr. Phipps was alone in his office when he heard a knock at the door. "Come in," he said.

He looked up from his desk. "Oh! Hello Manny. What can I do for you?"

"Hi, Mr. Phipps." Manny sat down a little awkwardly in a chair. "Do you remember inviting me to a God meeting?"

Mr. Phipps raised an eyebrow. "A God meeting?"

"Yeah," said Manny.

"Oh, you mean the Saturday morning Bible study for the older boys! Yes, of course. Are you interested?"

"Well, I've been talking to Sarah… uhm, Mrs. Marshall… you know, my new mom lady. She's been talking to me about Jesus and the love of God. Then, I remembered what you said."

"What I said?" Mr. Phipps interrupted.

"Yeah. You said that God loves me. Uhm, you said you would be praying that I'd find out that He loves me or something like that."

"Yes, of course. I remember now."

"Well, did you?" questioned Manny.

"Did I? Did I what?"

"Pray for me."

"Actually, yes. You were on my heart quite a bit around the time you met your new family. During that season, especially, I was praying for you daily. I think the Lord has answered those prayers, don't you?"

Manny said, "Yeah, well, uhm, can I come? On Saturday? I mean, I know I'm only here a few more…"

Mr. Phipps interrupted, "Manny, yes, you are welcome. Please join us. You know what, you could even keep coming after your adoption if you like. We meet early. 8:30 am sharp."

IT WAS PRECISELY three Saturdays later, and Manny entered Mr. Phipps' office at 8:30 am sharp. It was his third time attending the young men's Bible study. Mr. Phipps looked up from his notes to greet him.

"Good morning, Manny! Or should I call you Mr. Marshall? That was such a special hearing at the courthouse Wednesday. I must tell you a secret. It was one of my favorite adoption hearings of my career. Don't tell anyone."

"I won't. And you can call me whatever you like. My adopted mom keeps introducing me as Emmanuel."

"Oh, you will get used to that. It's a small price to pay to belong in a family. What did you all do after the ceremony?"

"We went home."

"Oh, really. No party. No celebratory dinner?"

"The party is coming up in a few weeks, so we can include my new grandparents. They're in Ireland. My mom said to invite you."

"Well, I'd be delighted. I look forward to meeting your grandparents."

"So do I. Sammy talks about them all the time."

A few weeks passed, and so the day of the adoption party came to the Marshall's house. Mr. Phipps arrived early and knocked on the door. Sarah enthusiastically received him at the front door, which had a banner over it. "Welcome home, Emmanuel." As Mr. Phipps entered the house, he saw the same banner draped over the living room, and across the back patio. He waved at Manny, who ran by him while chasing Sammy saying, "Come back here with that! Give it back!"

"They seem to be acting like true brothers already." He smiled with this comment toward Sarah.

"Yes. They are friends, but they are loud."

"You know, I've heard good things about your mom and dad, Sarah. I look forward to meeting them."

"Mr. Phipps, they look forward to meeting you, too. I've

told them so much about you. They should be here any minute."

Just then, Sammy ran back toward them with Manny not far behind. As Sammy sought momentary refuge from Manny's pursuit behind Sarah, he heard Phil say, "Ok, you two. That's enough! Sammy, take a drink of water. Let's wait for our guests, please." Phil greeted Mr. Phipps before sitting down on a nearby couch.

Just then, Sarah developed an idea to occupy Sammy as they waited for guests. "Sammy, I was just talking about your grandparents with Mr. Phipps. Can you tell him one of your stories about your grandpa? He will be here soon."

"I'd love to hear a story," said Mr. Phipps.

Sammy took a deep breath before pausing dramatically to start his story. "One day there was this dog."

Sarah interjected while making eye contact with Mr. Phipps. "Oh! This is his first memory of his grandpa. I've heard this one." Mr. Phipps smiled back at her while Sammy continued.

"Yeah, I was four years old. So, there was this dog…"

Sarah interrupted again, "Sammy, start the story before the dog part… maybe the church part first?"

"Oh yeah, ok. So, Grandpa wanted me to go to church with him. I think it was Sunday."

Everyone smiled.

"So, he gave me this little Bible with my name on it. It's in my room. My grandpa, he said 'Let's go', so we started walking. He wouldn't let me walk on my own, so I had to hold his hand. We walked down streets, you know."

Manny mentally noted the holding hands part, so he could tease his kid brother about that later. Sammy continued while looking at Sarah. Mr. Phipps was nodding along as if Sammy was looking directly at him.

"So, we walked like that for a while. There was this dog,

but Grandpa took me on the other side of the street, so the dog wouldn't bite me. I mean, uhm, I never saw the dog. He just did it just in case."

Manny blurted out, "So, there was no dog. That's boring."

Sarah clarified, "Well, actually, Sammy, Grandpa shifted you across the street, because he knew you were approaching a dog. He didn't want the dog to bark at you… uhm, I guess that's not a terribly interesting story. I'm sorry Mr. Phipps."

Mr. Phipps quickly replied while looking at Sarah. "Actually, that story tells me quite a bit about your dad's care for your son."

His words hung in the air for a few moments, and then Sammy let out a cheer as the doorbell rang.

"It's them! It's them!"

It was them. Judge O'Connell and Wemaw stood with other arriving party goers at the front door under the banner. Sarah opened the door as she found eight people waiting to meet Manny and party.

Manny stood back, now filled with excited anticipation. He watched intently as Sarah and Phil opened the door. The crush of humanity spilled into the house with joy-filled greetings, hugs, handshakes, and pats on the back. Knowing that he was the kid of the hour, Manny smiled at the people. His face shifted, though, when he saw an unwelcome guest.

"What's HE doing here?" Manny's mind grappled with the reality that Judge Frankenstein was coming through the door while hugging his new mother. "No! Go away!" Grandpa headed straight for Manny and extended his hand. "Hello, my boy. I'm Grandpa!"

Manny stared at that awful, scarred hand. The sight of it filled him with fear and dread, so Manny retreated. He walked backwards, banging into the wall behind him. He glanced around the room. All eyes were now on him. Phil said, “Hey, be careful!” and Sarah said, “Manny, be nice. That’s Grandpa!”

As Manny started to run, he heard Sammy say, “What’s wrong with Manny?” as he slipped through the crowd into the front yard. Manny was sprinting down the street before anyone could react. Phil took off after him, while Sarah began to make her way toward the front door. Before she could join the chase, Mr. Phipps called out to her.

“Mrs. Marshall, I know what this is about.”

Mr. Phipps had watched the whole scene play out. He saw the kindly judge walk through the door, becoming instantly delighted that such a man could be Manny’s new grandpa. Instantly, his impression turned to concern for how Manny would react. He watched Manny react with expected horror. Mr. Phipps then realized that only he would know why Manny could behave this way.

So, Mr. Phipps told Sarah what he knew. He described what happened in the courtroom, explaining that he and Manny had two very different reactions to the judge that day. He further explained that Judge O’Connell had come to symbolize to Manny the God that destroyed his family and one day would get him too. Finally, he said, “Manny has always called him Judge Frankenstein.”

11

OPPOSING VIEWS

Sarah began chasing after Phil, who was chasing after Manny. She suddenly stopped in her tracks. She turned back toward Henry Phipps. "Oh! Mr. Phipps, can you tell my parents what you just told me?"

Sarah then ran one block before she saw Phil walking in her direction with his arm locked around Manny.

"He won't tell me what's gotten into him." His wife side-hugged Manny, saying, "That's okay. I know."

Sarah explained the situation to Phil as the three walked back to the house. After receiving this explanation and as they approached their home, Phil looked at Sarah but spoke to Manny.

"Manny, just play with Sammy during the party. In time, you will see how much we all love you, including your grandfather. But, for today, we won't force you to talk with anyone. Ok?" Sarah's eyes communicated to her husband that she appreciated this approach.

Manny heartily agreed. "Ok."

But when Manny returned to Sammy's room, Sammy was in no mood to play.

"Hey, what's your problem? That's our grandpa! You don't need to be afraid of him. He's the nicest guy in the world. Why did you run away?"

"He's YOUR grandpa. Not mine. To me, he's scary. Ok? You don't know what I know about him."

"That's true. I know a lot MORE about him than you! You don't know him at all."

"He's a judge. I know that."

"So!?"

"Well, one time I did something wrong, and he was my judge, and he was mean, ok?"

"What did you do wrong?"

"Sammy! Argh! That's not the point. The point is… you have your ideas about him, and I have mine."

"But your ideas must be wrong if you're AFRAID of him! Have you ever spent time with him or talked with him? Have you ever played baseball with him? I have. How about pine toss? We play pine toss together. I KNOW him. I know what he's really like. You don't."

"Pine toss? What's that? Oh, never mind! Don't you see, Sammy? He treats you different. You're his grandkid!"

Sammy summoned courage. He looked right into Manny's eyes and said, "So are you."

Simultaneously, there was another conversation happening in the living room.

"I'm sorry, dear. I should have anticipated that this could happen. I know how kids look at me in teen court. I know I can seem scary." Grandpa's eyes darted back and forth from Sarah to Phil as he said these words.

"It's not your fault, Dad. We will work it out." She paused momentarily. "He will find out who you are over time. We have plenty of time. We just don't want to overwhelm him today."

"Yes, of course, I get that. Let's take it slow."

Wemaw overheard this conversation but then walked from the kitchen into the living room. She sat down in a chair near Mr. Phipps.

"Mr. Phipps, did you say Emmanuel calls my husband 'Judge Frankenstein'? Why?"

"Mrs. O'Connell, due to Manny's court case, which, you know, I was the one who accompanied him to your husband's courtroom... well, that was quite an experience for Manny, so we've had a few conversations about your husband."

"Oh. I see."

After a few moments, Mr. Phipps explained further. "Actually, I tried to explain to Manny that I thought your husband was very fair to him and treated him with kindness. But, you know, he was eleven at the time." He paused. "Yeah, eleven. He saw and interpreted everything as an eleven-year-old. The room, the robe, the scars. I believe your husband may have a scar on his hand?"

"Yes. He certainly does."

"So, that's the Frankenstein part. Mrs. O'Connell, Manny came to me once and described a dream he had. In his dream, 'Judge Frankenstein', as he puts it, sat in his elevated place in the courtroom while hurling lightning bolts out of his scar toward Manny."

"Oh dear!"

"Yes. I'm afraid his misunderstanding of who your husband is... well, and who God is for that matter... well, it's quite extreme."

"Yes. Poor boy. He's been through so much in his life. Thank you, Mr. Phipps, for explaining it to me. We must all do our part to undo these lies that he believes. In the end, it's love to speak the truth and correct misunderstandings, is it not?"

"It is, Mrs. O'Connell. It is."

She looked at him one last time. "You can call me Wemaw."

12

HE HIT A TEACHER

Over the next few days, Manny began dealing with the reality of his new world. He could not go on as he had before. Now, Judge Frankenstein was his grandfather. "I have a new mom, a new dad, and a new brother," Manny stated the obvious to himself. He then thought, "I have a new grandfather, and he's a monster. But, is he really a monster? Sammy, Mom, Dad… they all say 'no.' I won't be tricked, though. I must watch him closely."

So, that's what Manny did. He watched. As Sammy spent time with Grandpa, Manny watched. When they played catch in the backyard, Manny said "no, thank you" and watched. When Grandpa and Manny attended Sammy's soccer games, Manny watched Grandpa watching Sammy. He saw him smile. He saw him cheer. He saw him laugh. Whenever Grandpa arrived at the house, Sammy would cheer and hug him. Manny stood back. During the spring months, Sammy was the one who enjoyed Grandpa. Manny was the one who stood on the sideline and watched.

While Manny was watching, Lucas was plotting. He knew

he could not exact revenge on the former orphan in the boys' home, but perhaps he could at school. On the following Monday, Lucas executed the plan during the afternoon passing period.

Manny walked down the hallway on that Monday afternoon, thinking to himself and processing all that he had watched. "Maybe he's not such a bad guy," he thought. "Maybe I should give him a break and join in the fun like Sammy does." Manny put his science book in his locker while pulling out his math book. He walked toward his next class, trying to think more pleasant thoughts about his new grandfather.

Suddenly, Manny was attacked. Lucas thrust his forearm and launched all of his weight into Manny's chest, causing Manny to fall back into the lockers behind him. Lucas then whispered something into Manny's left ear that was so vile, it caused Manny to explode with anger.

Manny thrust Lucas to the ground, jumping on top of him. The other students in the hallway started yelling and gesturing. As Manny thrashed Lucas, Lucas inwardly rejoiced. His plan was working. It worked even better when a teacher heard the fracas and entered to break it up. Mrs. Borders reached, shouted while trying to get between them. At that moment, Manny's elbow thrust backward to punch Lucas once more, but connected instead with Mrs. Borders' nose. It was a violent blow. The force caused the teacher's nose to bleed, swelling instantly.

A few minutes later, Manny found himself waiting in a chair outside the principal's office.

He wasn't there long before he saw a man with a badge enter the small waiting room. The badged man asked Mrs. Haliburton to "please let Mr. McAnich know that Detective Allen has arrived." Detective Allen stood a few feet away from Manny as he awaited Mr. McAnich. Making eye contact, he said, "Hello, you must be Manny?"

"Yes sir."

Mrs. Haliburton's unpleasant voice broke through the awkward silence. "Detective, Mr. McAnich will see you now."

The detective didn't reply to Mrs. Haliburton but swiftly moved past Manny toward the interior office door now held open by the high school principal. The door closed decisively once the detective entered.

Manny looked up at Mrs. Haliburton. "Wow, I guess I'm really in trouble."

"Mmm-hmmm… you can't hit a teacher, dear."

Manny's mind then started to grapple with the gravity of his situation. "I hit a teacher. I not only pummeled Lucas, a fellow student, but somehow I must have hit Mrs. Borders. Oh no! I've really blown it. There's no recovery from this. I'll be arrested. I'm going to jail. Mrs. Haliburton is right, you can't hit a teacher! Oh God! What have I done? What about Mom? Dad? Sammy? They will all know what I've done! They'll send me back to the orphanage. Of course they will. I've only lived with them for a short while. Why not send me back? I'm not really one of them. Lucas has won. He's brilliant! I'm a fool."

Manny was so deep in somber thought and despair that he couldn't hear his new name being called by Mrs. Haliburton.

"Mr. Marshall? Mr. Marshall? Mr. Marshall!"

He finally heard when she said, "Manny!"

He did not reply but walked swiftly toward the interior office door, which was now open for him. He stepped through the door, which was then decisively closed behind him. The principal never spoke a word to him, but nodded at Detective Allen. Detective Allen told Manny that since he had struck a teacher causing bodily harm, he would be arrested for assault on a public servant. "That's a serious charge, Manny. Do you understand?"

"Yes sir."

"Come with me then."

Detective Allen placed Manny in the back seat of his unmarked police car and drove him to the County Juvenile Correction Center. Manny was booked into the facility. He then sat by himself in a small, closed, locked room with grey carpet and white walls. Now alone with his thoughts, he began to construct a new plan of survival for his return to the orphanage. "I can't be soft!" he thought. "I beat up Lucas, so that will help my reputation. I won't speak with Mr. Phipps or go to his Bible time. All of his talk of love and look where it's gotten me. I knew God would eventually get me. He must be laughing now. What a trick! It wasn't enough just to blast me with a lightning bolt. He taunted me with the promise of a new life, and I fell for it! I'm such a fool. First a lie, and then the lightning. Now I'm struck."

Then Manny became struck with a new kind of horror. He saw through the interior window of his holding cell the figure and face of the lightning bearer himself. Judge Frankenstein had surely come to collect him to deposit him back into the orphanage. Now, Manny could see that a large, uniformed man was coming toward his door. This man opened Manny's cell door while saying, "Mr. Marshall, come with me, please." Manny followed the uniformed officer, who asked him to sit down in the large room in the middle of the facility. This room was surrounded by all of the holding cells that contained kids like Manny. Manny had previously observed while being booked in the large open room, that the room contained various cubicles where uniformed and non-uniformed people busily worked.

As Manny sat down in his new seat, he could now see Judge Frankenstein across the room. Manny dared not make eye contact with him. However, Manny could now hear his voice as he spoke to another man.

"No, Sergeant, I'm not here to set anyone's bail today."

"No?"

"No, actually, the State of Texas doesn't allow a judge to set bail for his own grandson."

Curiously, the uniformed sergeant addressed the judge. "Oh? Who's your grandson?"

"Well, my grandson's name is Emmanuel Marshall… though the system may have him listed as Emmanuel Ortega. Would you mind grabbing his file? I'm here to pay his bond."

"Yes, sir. Of course."

Manny could overhear every word of this conversation. He thought. "He's here to pay my bond?" After signing his name several times, Manny found himself following his new grandpa through the kid-jail parking lot.

"This is my car. Please get in."

Manny climbed into the passenger seat. While clasping his seat belt, he said nervously, "Where are you taking me?"

"You HIT a teacher?"

"Are you taking me back to the orphanage?"

"I'm taking you to my house."

"What are you going to do with me?"

"What am I going to do? I am going back to work. My docket was interrupted by a call from Sarah, uhm, your mom, saying that you had been ARRESTED. I had to tell the clerk that I had to stop everything, so I could bail my grandson out of jail."

"Why are you taking me to YOUR house?"

"Your parents are at work. I'm not leaving you by yourself. Plus, I can't think of anyone more perfectly suited to deal with you right now than Wemaw. I mean, how could you have possibly HIT a TEACHER?"

"I'm not talking to you about it."

"After spending the afternoon with your grandmother, you will wish you had."

"Is that a threat?"

"It's a promise."

13

WEMAW SPILLS IT

Manny felt his heart race as he and Grandpa pulled into Grandpa's driveway. Grandpa turned around to look at Manny, saying in a frustrated tone, "I've got people waiting for me in the courtroom. I'm dropping you off here. I called Wemaw from the jail earlier to tell her I was bringing you home. Go in that front door there. She is expecting you."

Manny proceeded up the sidewalk defeatedly and knocked on the front door. He saw a pleasant-looking older woman answer the door. "Hi Emmanuel. Please come in."

She motioned toward the kitchen table, as Manny obediently sat down in a dining chair. Wemaw brought him a cold glass of water and put it in front of him on the table.

"I never thought I'd begin a conversation with my new grandson this way, but you HIT a TEACHER?"

Manny stammered, then spoke. "It was an accident. I was punching Lucas, and she caught my elbow with her face."

"Oh, I see. It was probably her fault then," Wemaw said sarcastically. Manny stared at her blankly.

"Well, I don't know what that's going to mean for you,

Emmanuel. It can't be good. But I don't want to talk about that. You've actually got bigger problems that we need to resolve, and we're going to do that right now."

Manny was now thoroughly confused. He thought to himself, "What could possibly be a bigger problem for a kid like me than facing school expulsion and potential jail time?"

She saw the confusion on his face. "The bigger problem you're facing concerns your grandfather."

"I knew it!" Manny thought. "She's going to tell me that I'm in danger."

Then Wemaw sat down at the table with Manny, looking him in the eye. Almost involuntarily, she reached out and touched his forearm, now squeezing it. She let go as she said, "Manny, I have something I should tell you. May I tell you a story? It's not really a story because it actually happened, but this will be difficult for me. You see, I've never told anyone this story before. I've never uttered it out loud."

"Well, you don't have to…" he interrupted.

But then she interrupted his interruption. "Manny, I'm going to tell you this story now. But first, we're going to pray together that I may tell it to you as I should." They both bowed their heads as Wemaw prayed aloud:

"Loving Lord, please be with my spirit as I tell my grandson about the events of July 18, 1988. I know you know this will be difficult for me, but Manny needs to know. So he can understand, I need to not cry or be emotional. Will you help me with that? Will you be my strength and inner peace as I tell it? In fact, Lord, I cannot. I ask that YOU tell it through me. As I pray, yes, that seems like the best way. I thank you in advance. For Your name's sake. Amen."

Manny looked up and looked at Wemaw with great, but frightful anticipation.

She said, "I'm sure I have your attention now, Manny."

"Yes, ma'am."

"Manny, I am your Wemaw now, and you should address me as..."

"Actually, you're my adopted..."

Wemaw once again interrupted with a slightly raised voice, "I am your Wemaw, Manny. Please address me by name in the future."

"Yes ma'am, uh, I mean, Wemaw."

"Manny, I want to talk with you about your grandpa's scar. I know that you know the one I mean. It stretches from his hand to his arm."

Manny nodded in amazement.

Wemaw once again looked Manny in the eye and began.

"Sarah was in high school, and it was her birthday. There was a stage production playing in San Antonio that she really wanted to see. She was so excited about this musical, Manny. So, we took her for her birthday. Yeah, so we made it a whole weekend celebration. We stayed in a hotel. She asked her best friend to be with us as a special treat. We all were so excited!

"Our hotel was only a few blocks from the theater, so we decided to walk to the show. After walking to the theater, we enjoyed a lovely event. In fact, after the show, we ran into some dear friends that we had not seen in a long time. We visited with them for probably thirty minutes. That was wonderful, but we paid a price for that visit, Manny. Since we stayed so long after the show, all the spectators had left the theater, so the streets had emptied out. Of course, we thought nothing of it. We just started walking back to the hotel.

"About a block from the theater, we were startled when an attacker approached us with a long-bladed knife. He was so scary. I'll never forget what he looked like. I'll never forget the terrible things he screamed at us as he lunged at your... well, as he lunged at us. At that point, your grandfather..."

Unwisely, Manny interrupted, "He's my adopted..."

"No!" Wemaw snapped. "He is your grandpa! Do you understand? I would not tell you this story otherwise."

"Ok, Wemaw. Ok."

"Manny, I'm sorry. I'm sorry." She began to weep. She then took a deep breath and, after a few moments, began again.

"Your grandfather was so brave. He stepped in front of the attacker, taking a blow from the knife across his hand and forearm. He fought bravely against the man until some passersby came to assist him. Because of your grandpa's actions, I was not hurt. Neither was your… neither was Sarah. Neither was her friend."

Manny, now looking at Wemaw with wide eyes, muttered, "Whoa, that's how he got that scar?"

"Yes, that's how he got that scar. He has others too, Manny. You will never see them, but he has other scars as well. He was in the hospital for several days afterward. We weren't sure if he would survive the attack. Of course, I stayed by his side. Once, while we were alone, I thanked him for stepping in and saving us all. Do you know what he said?"

Manny, still wide-eyed, looked at her, shaking his head.

"He said, 'Don't you know? My dear, I love you so much. There's nothing I wouldn't do to protect you and our family.'"

Wemaw paused to look at Manny. She then spoke. "Our family. Now, I've thought about that word family over the past few days, you know. Our family. Our family on that day consisted of myself, Sarah, and Sarah's best friend."

Wemaw looked at Manny intently. "So, do you know who Sarah's best friend was?"

Manny reflected Wemaw's gaze and proudly proclaimed, "My mother."

"Yes, Manny. It was your mother. She was part of our family that day. Actually, your mom and Sarah were very close, so they spent lots of time together at our house. So, your mom felt like part of our family on many days. But, yes, Emma was with us that day, and your grandpa's scar is proof that she was protected. We all were." Wemaw sighed, took a deep breath before continuing.

"So, do you see why I felt I should tell you that story? You deserve to know the truth. You would probably never hear it from him."

"I see. I was wrong about him. Wemaw, I called him Judge Frankenstein. I thought he was out to get me." He paused a few moments while she patted his arm. He whispered, "I couldn't have been more wrong."

"That's ok, Manny. We are family, don't you see? I hope that you can trust that from now on. We aren't out to get you. We want to love you… make you feel a part of us. You are one of us. That's how we feel. Ok?"

"Ok."

"Well, I don't know about you, but I'm exhausted. Would you like a Coke?"

Manny didn't respond. After a few moments of silence, he smiled, saying, "Wemaw, I have an idea."

Wemaw listened as Manny explained the idea. When he finished, she reacted with a smile. She then gave her grandson a warm hug and said, "I like it."

Mr. Phipps was in his office working late that Monday afternoon. His phone rang. He answered and said, "Well, hello Manny! How are you? Oh, mm hmm. Is that alright with your grandparents? Mm hmm. Oh! I see. Well, yes, I can do that. What's the address?"

Approximately fifteen minutes later, Mr. Phipps pulled into Wemaw's driveway, and saw Manny at the front door.

Manny climbed into Mr. Phipps' backseat before they drove away together.

During the ride, Manny told Mr. Phipps about the unfortunate incident at school. Mr. Phipps involuntarily blurted out, "You HIT a TEACHER!?" Manny further explained the situation, and then they arrived at the courthouse. The car came to a stop at the entrance curb. Manny thanked Mr. Phipps for the ride, then exited the vehicle. He started walking up the exterior stairs toward the large wooden doors. He took a deep breath before proceeding through the hallways that led to the courtroom. It all seemed very familiar to him, but now the place had a different feel. He wasn't ashamed. He wasn't afraid. As he entered the large courtroom, he noticed that it was mostly empty but for a smattering of lawyers and nervous-looking people. Manny intentionally sought out the same seat from his previous visit and sat down. Grandpa was seated on the bench as he saw his grandson sit down in the fourth row. Judge O'Connell had difficulty concentrating for the next thirty minutes before eventually concluded the hearing. After dismissing the parties, the Judge motioned for Manny to come through a certain door back to his chambers.

Still clothed in his robe, Grandpa unlocked the door to greet his grandson. "Hey, I'm glad you're here. Follow me to my office." Manny obediently followed his grandpa down the hall until they made a right turn into the office. It was a large office, and Manny stayed near the door while Grandpa walked toward his office desk. As Grandpa started to unzip his robe, he said, "Manny, I'm glad you're here, but how did you get here? Uhm, what are you doing here?"

Before he could get all of these words out, Grandpa could no longer see Manny. Instead, he FELT Manny. Manny had his arms wrapped around his grandpa's midsection. Grandpa returned the embrace, while Manny was draped in the folds of his robe.

Manny felt at home with this man as he felt tightly squeezed. The black robe felt good and smelled good. Manny was just about to release his grip when he felt the presence of another. How strange, but yes, now Manny was being hugged from behind as he hugged Grandpa in front. The hug sandwich concluded, as Manny turned around. He couldn't believe his eyes.

14

HUG SANDWICH, PART TWO

For Sarah, that same day had begun with a prayer of thanksgiving. It was her custom to roll out of bed each morning to start the day by talking to God. To her, He was more than a deity. He was her Father and she was His child. She began:

"Father, good morning. Even though it's Monday and I have a long day of work caring for patients, I know You desire to be with me. You really are good, aren't You? It's been dawning on me how, in Your goodness, You are able to accomplish so much. I remember my tirade prayer several months ago after I had the tornado dream. I was angry, wasn't I? I was really mad at You. Looking back now, I can see how You have put the pieces together. I mean, You've given us a SON! You connected the dots between our family, Emma's, the tornado, and Manny. I pleaded with You to connect the dots, and You DID. Phil and I asked You to give Sammy a sibling, and You DID. We put our faith in You. You came through so beautifully. Thank You, Father. What a beautiful redemption story You have written here. Now, we get to live it out. How wonderful is that? I'm overwhelmed with Your goodness.

"Saying so, I must persist with one more request that's on my heart. There is this matter of Manny and my dad. Father, the party was ROUGH. Manny was scared, our guests were confused, and my parents must have been hurt...at least a little. I mean, Judge Frankensein? I never saw that coming. I would love for You to resolve this... this... this misunderstanding. Someday, I would love for Manny to see my dad as Sammy sees him. That seems like a tall order, but I know You can do it. It's just a matter of perception, but isn't that why You sent Jesus? To change our perception of You? To let us see You as Jesus does? Ok, I've got to get in the shower, but that's my prayer this morning. Take me with You today. For Your name's sake. Amen"

A few hours later, while Sarah was talking with a patient, she heard a knock at the door of the examination room. Annoyed at this interruption, Sarah excused herself to open the door, expecting a nurse. Instead, she was surprised to see a member of the administrative staff hand her a note while saying, "Dr. Marshall, I'm so sorry to interrupt you, but your son's school called. Uhm, they need you to call them as soon as you can." Now alarmed, Sarah thanked the messenger, and went back to her patient. Approximately ten minutes later, Sarah called the number written on the note. She said, "Hello, this is Sarah Marshall. I was told to call about my son? Is this about Sammy or Manny? Oh, I see. Wait! He what?! Manny HIT a TEACHER? He's where? Oh no! How do I get to him? Oh, Lord, what do I do? Ok, yes ma'am. I understand you. Where is that place? The juvenile center, I mean. I see. Yes, I know that part of town. Alright. Oh, I just can't believe this. Please tell Mrs. Borders I am so sorry. Can I help with her nose? No, of course, you're right... probably not appropriate… oh, how embarrassing. I am so sorry. Yes. Goodbye."

Sarah took a deep breath before praying a different kind of prayer. "Oh Father, what do I do? I'm in the middle of rounds. I have patients to see. Oh! Like Mrs. Tolbert… she needs me! Phil is out of town on a work site, and…"

Just as the words "on a work site" spilled out of her mouth, her dad's face came to mind. "Yes, of course! He knows the criminal justice system… he will know what to do. Does he have a docket today? Oh, I don't know!"

Sarah took a chance and called her dad's office. The phone was answered by the court clerk, who said, "Oh no dear, he is on the bench right now." Sarah had known Dotty Madsen for many years. Dotty had worked with Judge O'Connell for many years. She was a trusted family friend. Sarah shared with Dotty what she knew of the situation. Afterward, Dotty promised to scribble a note, so she could slip it to the bailiff. The bailiff slipped the note to Judge O'Connell, who paused the courtroom proceedings in order to call his daughter back.

After a short conversation with Sarah, Grandpa assured her that he would take care of the boy. He said, "Try not to worry. I'll be in touch."

As hard as she tried, Sarah found it difficult to concentrate on her patients. During a break, she called Phil. He offered to drive back to Poplarton, and Sarah agreed that would be best. On her lunch break, she called her dad's phone, which was, again, answered by Dotty Madsen. Sarah was relieved to hear Dotty say that her dad had delivered Manny safely into Wemaw's care at their house after bailing him out of jail.

"Ok," she thought. "I only have a few more patients after lunch. Then I'll head over there to see him."

"Lord, what do I say? What has happened?"

At precisely 2:47 pm, Sarah Marshall left the clinic, racing toward her mother and her son. Frazzled in mind, Sarah knocked on the door as she entered her parents' front door. "Mom? Manny?!"

Seeing Wemaw, she exclaimed. "Mom! Hi! Where is he? What's happened? He HIT a TEACHER?!"

"Hello, dear. He's not here, but he's in a good place now."

"What do you mean? Where is he?"

"Sarah, dear, calm down. He went with Mr. Phipps to see Grandpa."

Utterly baffled, Sarah replied, "But I thought he was here. Why would he go to Dad again? Mom, what's happened?"

"Sarah, I told him."

"You told him? You told him what?"

Wemaw touched Sarah's arm as she touched Manny's before. She looked into her daughter's eyes saying, "I told him. He knows the story behind the scars now. He KNOWS. And now, he wants to be with him."

"I see," said Sarah as tears welled up in her eyes.

"Emmanuel was quite moved and called Mr. Phipps. I don't have my car today, so Manny called Mr. Phipps. He agreed to give Manny a ride to the courthouse. They left about ten minutes ago."

As Sarah proceeded toward the front door, Wemaw understood why she must leave and where she was going. She told her daughter of Manny's criminal charges, explaining what had happened at school that day.

Now reeling with disappointment, Sarah drove toward her dad and her son. "I've got to remember to reimburse Dad for the bail money. Surely, he will be expelled from school. Dad can tell us what to expect in Manny's criminal case. Will he go back to jail?" These thoughts elevated Sarah's blood pressure as she drove. "He can't do things like this. Did he behave this way at the boys' home?" She walked quickly across the parking lot after exiting the car. "He's going to know I'm angry. Where is he?"

Sarah's eyes peered intently around every door and every corner, ready to unleash her disappointment on the boy. He was nowhere to be found. She entered the courtroom but found it empty. "Where is he? There! There is Dotty!" She spied the clerk in an adjacent hallway, and they locked eyes.

"Hi, can you buzz me in?"

"Hi, there! Of course! They're in his office, I think."

As Sarah walked down the hall, she could see the office door. Would she apologize to her dad first or fuss at Manny for what he had done? Her heartbeat racing, she entered the office. What she saw next melted her. They were locked in an embrace. Her dad's arms locked around her boy's shoulders. Her boy's arms locked around her dad's robed middle. None of the day's events mattered now. Her stress. Manny's guilt. She need not apologize. She need not fuss. There was only one thing left to do. She chose to join her dad as the bread in a tight hug sandwich. Her morning prayer flashed across her mind as Manny looked up at her. The hug resumed as Manny remained smack in the middle.

15

AFTER EFFECTS

On the following Saturday, Ralph and Sadie, a couple in their seventies, were out for breakfast at a Poplarton café. After breakfast, Ralph escorted his wife across the parking lot to open the car door for her. He climbed into the driver's seat and said, "Well, what did you think?"

"The toast was dry."

Ralph, ignoring her comment, asked, "Could you hear the conversation at the table next to us?"

"You were a fly on the wall? I thought you were listening to me."

While driving, Ralph glanced in his wife's direction. "You literally didn't say one word during breakfast."

"We've been married for 51 years. What is there to say?" she said with a grin.

"Well, the conversation next to us was interesting."

"You mean the old man, the younger man, and the kid?"

"Yes, I think it was a grandfather, a dad, and a young man. They talked like family, but none of them looked alike."

"Right. Well, what did they say?" asked Sadie.

"At first, it seemed like they were coming up with a strategy for the young man's legal troubles.

"The dad would ask the grandpa-guy questions, and then Grandpa would talk about what might happen."

"That's not interesting."

"Right, but then Grandpa seemed to dismiss the need to discuss the legal matter. He started talking about Jesus."

Sadie raised an eyebrow while saying, "I bet he did. Like a warning to the kid? If he doesn't straighten up, Jesus will be watching his every move?"

"No, the old man started reading Bible verses. They were Bible verses quoting Jesus. 'Love your enemy. Pray for those who persecute you.' That sort of thing. He must have read four verses along those lines."

"He got his Bible out at the table and read it to the kid?"

"Yes, right there next to us. I'm surprised you didn't see him."

"Oh yes, with my 20-20 vision," quipped Sadie as she peered through her thick eyeglasses.

"Anyway, the kid bristled at this a bit, but then the grandpa said something that struck me."

"Oh?"

"Yes, he said, 'There's no need to fear. You are loved. Your dad and I are FOR you.' And then the dad-guy put his arm around the kid. He said, 'I'll be right there with you.'"

Ralph continued to speak while making a right turn onto Goodwin Street. "Anyway, it wasn't WHAT was said exactly, but there was something about how they were talking that touched me."

"Actually, I can tell that you're a little emotional. What's wrong with you?"

With a tear in his eye, Ralph concluded, "Those three really loved each other. I don't know. The omelet may have given me heartburn."

~

APPROXIMATELY TWO HOURS LATER, Lucas was outside performing assigned chores on the grounds of the boys' home. He looked up and saw someone approaching.

"What is HE doing here?" Lucas thought to himself, and then he said to the approaching kid, "Hey loser, I knew they'd bring you back. I guess they didn't really want you, did they? Welcome back where you belong."

Manny said, "Hey Lucas, I'm here to apologize. Uhm, I shouldn't have hit you in the hall."

Lucas' jaw dropped, as Manny continued.

"Here, I brought you some candy. You like Twizzlers, right?"

As the boys were talking, Phil watched alongside Mr. Phipps from his office window. To break the tension, Phil said, "Hey, do you have any popcorn?"

Finding no humor in the situation, Mr. Phipps stared out the window and said, "This is remarkable. What are those? Twizzlers?"

Lucas received the offered candy as burning coals upon his head.

"Listen loser, just because you're moving back in here, you must think you can buy some peace with candy. No way! You probably poisoned it. No! I'm going to make your life a living hell in here."

As Lucas moved toward Manny, Phil got up from his chair and moved past Mr. Phipps toward the office door.

"Lucas, you don't understand. I'm not moving back here. I'm only here to see you, you know, try to make up. I'd like us to be friends. I'll never live here again. I belong to a family now, and they love me. They'll never give me up, no matter what I do. It was my grandpa's idea for me to come see you.

Can we be friends? I'm tired of fighting, aren't you?" Manny extended his hand.

These words sent Lucas into a rage. He ran toward Manny, screaming. Phil acted in a flash, and ran forward, situating himself in between the two boys, acting as a shield for Manny while receiving Lucas' blows on his back. As Lucas screamed, Phil pleaded with Lucas to stop hitting them. Manny shouted as loud as he could toward Lucas. "Go to Mr. Phipps!! Go see him!! He's a good man, Lucas! You can trust him! Lucas, please. Mr. Phipps will take care of you!"

As Phil picked up Manny and carried him toward the parking lot, Mr. Phipps sat stunned at what he had seen. "Remarkable," he muttered. "I should go talk to Lucas. Lord, I need you."

16

THE PEOPLE

The next day, Sammy and Manny were taking advantage of the new basketball hoop Phil installed over the garage. Clang! Bmmp!

"Sammy, try to keep it from hitting the car!"

"Try not to miss so badly! Hey, Grandpa and Wemaw are coming over. Are you going to run away?"

"Shut up. That joke is getting old. You know I'm not."

Swoosh. "Good shot."

"Sorry about the joke. I'm glad you know him now. I tried to tell you he's not a monster."

"I know. I'm glad he's my Grandpa." Clang. "Hey, grab it!"

"Anyway, I wish everyone could have a Grandpa like him. He's great."

Sammy replied, "Here he is now!"

Grandpa and Wemaw exited the car. Wemaw warmly hugged each boy and said, "Hello, darlin'." Grandpa grabbed the basketball, throwing it to Sammy, "Let me see your moves." As Sammy gleefully took the basketball and shot layups and jump-shots, Grandpa took Manny aside and placed his hand on Manny's shoulder.

"Manny, your dad told me about what happened with Lucas. I can't tell you how proud of you I am. I thank God for you. No… Really, I do. It's one thing to hear the words of Jesus or to see them written on the page. It's quite another thing to do what He says. He was with you yesterday. I hope you felt His presence. Oh! And one more thing, Manny. He's proud of you, too."

After speaking these words, he signaled Sammy for the ball and shot it from ten feet away.

SWISH. "Good shot, Grandpa!"

"Are you boys up for a game of HORSE?"

Sammy shouted, "Oh, YES!!!"

"Sure," said Manny.

Fifteen minutes later, the boys came in for a drink and walked into Sammy's room. "I can't believe he beat us."

"Yeah, I should have told you. He's an old guy, but he's still good at sports."

"Well, now I know for myself," said Manny.

"Hey Manny, when you said you wished he could be everyone's grandpa? Yeah, I've thought about that. I kinda feel sorry for people… uhm, you know, I always hear people call him 'Judge' or 'Judge O'Connell', or there's another one… oh yeah! 'Your honor'. He's got all these names, you know?"

"Yeah! Or 'Judge Frankenstein'."

"Ha! Yeah. I feel kinda bad for the people who don't really know him like we get to know him. You know?"

"The people?"

"Yeah, the people."

This term struck the boys as funny. The people. They laughed.

Sammy's face lit up, and then he said, "C'mon!"

Sammy ran into the living room, followed closely by Manny. "Here! The people!" Sammy said as he laughed and pointed at a portrait of his grandpa on the mantle. "This is who they think he is." The portrait showed Judge O'Connell dressed in his robe, seated on his bench, hands folded with a stern look on his face.

Manny didn't laugh. He just looked at the portrait for five seconds, saying nothing. His face grew serious.

Sammy, still enthused, said, "Ok, c'mon!! C'mon Manny!" Sammy started running again, but toward his parents' room. Manny trotted after him. Suddenly, he didn't like this game. Manny's mood changed, though, when Sammy proudly pointed to a different picture and said, "THIS is him. The him that WE get. That's Grandpa."

Sammy pointed toward a small, framed photo of Sarah's dad on her bedside table. The photo showed him smiling broadly and wearing a hat. He seemed delighted, and all lit up inside.

Manny himself smiled broadly, laughed, and said, "Yeah. That's the guy that can beat you at HORSE." A few seconds went by, and then Manny said, "Yeah. I like that guy."

At that moment, Sarah walked into the bedroom and said, "Hey, what are you guys doing? I've been looking for you. Let's go! Get your shoes back on. Your grandparents want to take us out to eat."

Approximately one hour later, the family was seated at a table in a local café. The server came by, putting down their desired drinks in front of them. Just then, the boys saw Grandpa stand up to greet a man with a badge coming over to say hello.

The badged man said, "Well, hello Your Honor. You have quite a crew with you, I see."

Sammy looked quickly at his brother and said in a delighted whisper, "The people." Manny wanted to laugh, but Grandpa was busy proudly introducing everyone to the man. So, Manny had to hold it in.

This was the first occasion of many to come where the

grandsons would alternate saying "the people" to each other after their grandpa was greeted with one of his monikers in their presence.

On this occasion, Manny felt gratitude to his kid brother for helping him see that he was on the inside now. He's no longer one of "the people." Now, he is family. Now, he's the grandson.

DURING THE FOLLOWING WEEK, Manny was still suspended from school. He was bored at the house, but received a call on Thursday that he and his parents should report to his principal's office the next day at noon. He conveyed this news to Sarah and Phil, and they became cautiously optimistic that such a meeting could be a good thing. Sarah called her dad, and Grandpa came over soon after dinner on Thursday night. When Grandpa arrived, he sat down in the living room with Phil, Sarah, and Manny. Sarah explained that they had been summoned to see Mr. McAnich.

"Ok, that may or may not be good," said Grandpa. "As I've said before, Assault of a Public Servant is a felony, and it's a very serious charge... even for a kid." Manny nodded and tried to look unafraid. Grandpa continued.

"It's really going to come down to the teacher who was struck. If she wants to see this through, then the DA will most likely seek an indictment against Manny."

"I've heard she's still pretty mad," said Manny. "Timmy told me her nose doesn't look right."

"And that's another thing," Grandpa interjected. "She may want to sue to pay for a fixed nose."

Silence followed while everyone looked at each other. Grandpa continued.

"We may need to face the reality that this meeting with

the principal could be to inform Manny that he's been expelled. In fact, that would be my guess."

Phil then bravely prayed that the Lord's will would be done at the next day's meeting and that He would give them all courage to face whatever was next.

Afterward, Sammy looked over at his big brother and gravely shook his head. Manny gave Sammy a slight punch in the arm.

On the following day, Phil, Sarah, and Manny squeezed into the principal's waiting room and stared at Mrs. Haliburton, who stared right back at them.

After several minutes, her desk phone rang and she spoke briefly. She announced, "Mr. McAnich will see you now. You may go in."

The somber family (less Sammy) made their way into the principal's roomy office. They were greeted by Mr. McAnich, but each of them became disturbed when Detective Allen stood up and said "hello."

The principal motioned to Detective Allen's table and said, "Let's all gather around the table." Sarah noticed that there was still one unoccupied chair at the table. Just then, there was a knock at the door, and Mr. McAnich said, "Come on in, Mrs. Borders."

Manny's mind raced. "Mrs. Borders? What is SHE doing here?" Manny looked down so as to not to make eye contact with his victim.

Sarah spoke immediately and said, "Mrs. Borders, I'm Manny's mom, and please let me say just how very sorry we are for what has happened."

Mrs. Borders made direct eye contact with Sarah. "Thank you, Dr. Marshall."

Phil thought to himself, "Oh, she knows Sarah is a doctor. She's going to sue us for sure."

Mr. McAnich began the meeting. "Marshall family, I've

asked you to meet with us here today because there has been a development in Manny's situation. Detective Allen, would you please provide the details?"

"Yes, yes, of course. During this past week, I continued my investigation into the criminal case by contacting the victim, that is, uhm... the OTHER victim involved. Upon arriving at the boys' home, I met with Lucas Stevenson, and he told me some interesting things. Well, uhm, he let me know that he intentionally started the fight with Manny in order to get him into trouble. Lucas said that he never dreamed that a teacher would get punched in the fight, explaining to me that he was sorry and wished the whole thing had never happened."

Phil, Sarah, and Manny simultaneously raised their eyebrows in amazement. They looked at each other, and then Phil's lightbulb came on. "Mr. Phipps," he whispered.

"Mr. Phipps," Manny repeated under his breath.

Mr. McAnich then looked at Mrs. Borders.

She then addressed the group. "Manny, there's been another development."

Manny still refused eye contact.

"Manny, look at me," she said. He obeyed, and she continued.

"I'm not mad at you anymore. I have realized over the past few weeks that your behavior was bad, but I acted foolishly as well. A teacher with my years of experience should know better than to stick my nose between two fighting boys. I know you didn't know I was there and you never meant to strike me."

Detective Allen interrupted:

"Yes, well, I've spoken with the District Attorney's office about this matter, and I think we may be able to work it out. In exchange for some community service hours, and the payment of Mrs. Borders's medical bills."

"Just the doctor who treated my nose," interjected Mrs. Borders while gesturing toward her own face. "As you can see, I won't need plastic surgery or anything. I'll just call this my little Manny bump."

Detective Allen continued, "So, yes, in exchange for these things, the DA is willing to drop all charges."

There was a slight eruption of cheers, but Sarah interrupted, asking Mr. McAnich, "Does this mean that Manny can return to school?"

Smiling, Mr. McAnich looked back at Sarah. "Yes, ma'am, that's what it means."

Mrs. Haliburton, seated outside the room, could not quite make out what was being said inside the room despite her best efforts to do so. However, she could hear when the whole room rejoiced with a celebratory roar, and she shook her head with disapproval.

17

A CRISIS OF FAITH

On the following Sunday, the boys were at church. Manny sat in the fourth row between his grandparents. Sammy sat between Wemaw and his parents. Sammy liked singing the songs, taking communion, and listening to the sermon. He genuinely liked it. He liked these things because he loved his family. He loved how it felt to sit between Wemaw and his dad. He loved that his mom was sitting next to his dad. He could hear her sing the songs. He loved her voice. Strangely, Sammy also loved the mint ritual. He knew that each Sunday, his mother would pass him a mint during the sermon and pat his knee. Week after week, this sweet family ritual was Sammy's reality. He loved being loved. Further, he loved being together in close proximity with those who loved him.

When the Marshalls arrived home after church, the members of the family went to their rooms to change out of their church clothes into something more comfortable. After changing, Manny wandered into Sammy's room. "Hey, do you like church?"

"Yeah! I love it! Hey, does Mom ever give you a mint?"

"A mint? No. Why do you like it? I'm not sure I like what they say about God. I'm getting Judge Frankenstein vibes."

Sammy thought a few more moments than usual before answering one of his brother's questions.

"I like Grandpa's singing voice. I like it when Dad puts his arm around me during the sermon. Oh! And Mom usually gives me a mint and pats my knee. So, you really don't get a mint?"

"No. I sit way down from you by Grandpa, remember? She can't pass it that far."

"Oh right! Well, maybe next week we can trade so you can get one."

"Sammy, I don't care about the mint! Do you ever hear what they say about God?"

"Well, yeah. I've been going there longer than you. Uhm, I like what they say about Jesus. Yeah. I like Jesus. He came to save us from God, right? He was born on Christmas... all that stuff."

"Ok. Maybe I'll ask Dad. I've got some questions." After a moment's pause, Manny continued. "Have they ever told you if God sends tornadoes?"

"Yeah. That's a good question. Ask Dad. I think they think so at church. Tornadoes, lightning bolts... Yeah, stuff like that... you know... when He's mad. Hey, toss me my flip-flop."

Noticeably bothered that Sammy didn't seem as interested in his questions, he firmly tossed him his flip-flop. "It's just that I thought maybe I was wrong about God, like I was wrong about Grandpa."

"Oh yeah, definitely. Grandpa's coming over later. Did you know that?"

"Yeah, we're going to the movies."

Sammy burst out. "The movies!"

"So, is God good like Grandpa is good?"

"Ha, no! I mean, God's good. At church, they say He's good. But, no. Not like Grandpa. We get to hang out with Grandpa, and he likes us! Movies!!"

An hour later, Manny walked into his parents' room, flopped onto their bed, while asking, "Is God good?"

Phil and Sarah stopped their Sunday afternoon cleaning chores and looked at each other as if to say, "Do you want to answer that one?"

Phil tried a light-hearted approach. "Manny, your Grandpa will be here in fifteen minutes to take you and your brother out to a movie. What does THAT tell you about the goodness of God?" Phil smiled at his son.

Manny gave a half-hearted grin, as Sarah came over to sit on the bed. She looked into his face, "Emmanuel, your mom knew that God is good. Emma once told me that 'the Father of Jesus Christ is our Father, and He is good. We will never get to the end of His goodness. Whatever our view of God is, and no matter how good we think He is, He's better.'"

Manny's face softened but then stiffened. "Do you believe she was right? What about, you know… what about…"

"The tornado?" interjected Phil.

"Yeah."

Once again, Manny's parents looked at each other.

Phil answered, "Manny, that tornado is a part of your story. No doubt about that. It's a part of our story too. I really wish I could explain why we must suffer these things in this life. I wish I could explain the destructive forces of nature, Manny, but I can't. Tornadoes are not good. They are destructive and deadly. I'm so very sorry for the heartbreak and suffering you have gone through because of that terrible night. To answer your question, I believe that God is constantly working to redeem the bad stuff that happens to us here. He's still writing your story, Manny. Despite the tornado, you are still alive. He is writing your story. He loves you and wants you to know how it feels to be loved by Him. He is good because He is love."

As Manny wiped away a tear, he could hear distant yelling. He could tell that his kid brother was running down the hall, proclaiming, "He's here. He's here!"

Manny felt his parents' bed shake violently as Sammy launched himself through the air, landing six inches from Manny's face. Manny then heard the front door open as a familiar voice announced his presence with, "Hey boys, who's ready for the movies?"

As Grandpa was driving Manny and Sammy to the movies, he could sense their excitement. They were getting close to the theater as their car approached the intersection of Oakmont St. and Ninth Avenue.

"Boys, is this the first sequel or the second? Are there any reviews on IDMB?" Grandpa chuckled at his intentional mispronunciation of the acronym knowing he would soon be corrected by a grandson. But, the correction never came. No one in the car saw the red light runner enter the intersection until it was too late.

Upon impact, all of their car's safety equipment effectively deployed in an instant. The seatbelts and airbags kept all passengers safe from serious injury. However, Manny suddenly felt a sharp pain in his right arm. The front of the other car had rammed into the back right side of Grandpa's car, causing Grandpa's car to spin into a nearby light pole. When Manny's door collided with the light pole, his window shattered. As a result, a large shard of glass sliced his arm and embedded itself into his bicep just above the elbow. Manny screamed with pain as the car came to rest approximately fifty yards from the intersection.

Judge O'Connell quickly assessed the situation and realized he, himself, was unhurt. It soon became obvious that Manny was injured. He looked back at Sammy, who looked at him with awe and wonder as if he had just been on a theme park ride. "You ok?"

"Yep!"

Now Grandpa knew that he could turn all of his attention to Manny. "Ok. I see it. You've got quite a gash there." Manny writhed in anguish as Grandpa said, "Manny, listen. Turn your arm toward me, so I can help." Manny obeyed, then Grandpa carefully and quickly gripped the protruding glass shard between his index finger and thumb. He gripped the glass shard and pulled it out of Manny's arm.. As Manny cried out in agony, Grandpa dropped the shard onto the floorboard in front of him. Manny's wound needed instant attention. Grandpa placed his hand over Manny's wound tightly while applying pressure. Manny leaned into the pressure, but Grandpa quickly realized from the immense flow of blood coming out of the wound that Manny needed a tourniquet. Grandpa quickly looked around the car, but saw nothing that he could tie above the wound.

At that time, the other driver stumbled toward them shouting, "I'm sorry! I'm sorry sir! I think that was my fault."

"Not now! Call 911!" Grandpa yelled as he began to take off his own shirt. Sammy's eyes widened to see such a scene play out before him. Grandpa quickly ripped off a long sleeve from his own shirt. Sammy's eyes grew wider. Grandpa wrapped the torn off shirt-sleeve tightly just above the wound several inches below Manny's shoulder. "It's a deep cut, Manny, but help is on the way." While saying this, Grandpa applied pressure to Manny's wound with the remainder of his shirt in his hand. Manny then heard his grandfather pray aloud:

"Loving Lord, we need you more than ever. Send the

ambulance to us quickly. Preserve my grandson's arm. Help me know what to do to take care of my boy."

Sammy's joy ride experience diminished now as he saw his grandpa's blood-soaked shirt pressed against Manny's arm. "Grandpa, is Manny ok?"

"He's losing some blood... Sammy, do me a favor, watch for the ambulance. Let me know when you see it coming, ok?"

Sammy's eyes looked toward the street, while Manny's eyes looked toward Grandpa. He could see concern in his eyes, but a reassuring smile on his face. As Grandpa moved around with his shirt off, Manny could now see a scar on his back, which he presumed was caused by the attacker from many years ago.

"Hey Grandpa, I'm going to have a scar like you."

Manny said nothing else until he was revived by a nice lady inside his ambulance. "Manny, can you hear me? We're on our way to the hospital. You're going to be okay. We're taking good care of you."

"Ok," said Manny.

When Manny arrived at Mercy Regional Hospital, his arm was immediately cleaned and stitched up by one of the emergency room doctors. He was given fluids and continued to come back to himself as he rested comfortably in a recovery room distant from the hustle and bustle of the ER.

Grandpa, Sammy, Wemaw, Phil, and Sarah were all eager to see their beloved Emmanuel, but something happened to Manny in that room before they arrived. On the wall adjacent to Manny's recovery bed was a large ornate wooden frame that contained a scripture. The black words of the scripture were large, popping out of the white canvas. His eye kept coming back to these handwritten words:

He heals the brokenhearted and binds up their wounds (healing their pain and comforting their sorrow).

-- Psalm 147:3

MANNY STARED AGAIN and again at the contents of the frame. The words touched him deep, deep inside. After his parents, Grandparents and kid brother came, visited, and went back to the waiting room, Manny stared at these words again.

"Who is the 'He'?" he thought. "It must be God." Manny then looked over at his wounded arm and whispered to himself. "I have a wounded arm that is healing now. I also have some wounds nobody can see."

Manny bowed his head as a tear came to his eye. Continuing the whisper, he said:

"God, I thought You were Judge Frankenstein. I thought You were out to get me. I thought maybe Jesus came to save us from You. But maybe that's not true? God, if You are here, I hope You are what these words say You are. Is it true? Can You heal my broken heart? Can You bind up my unseen wounds?"

18

A DAY IN THE LIFE

Four months later, Manny was back in the courtroom. This time, he was there at the invitation of his Grandpa. It was a glorious summer day. The day began with Grandpa driving Manny to the courthouse early in the morning. Manny was introduced to the district clerk, who had provided breakfast tacos to the court staff. They were delicious. Grandpa told him where to sit and watch as Judge O'Connell conducted a few hearings. After a light morning docket, Manny was told by Grandpa that they were headed to lunch. As they entered the local café, it became obvious that they would not be eating alone. Manny sat at a table with Judge Grandpa, the court reporter, two attorneys, and one bailiff. Manny would later tell Sammy about how these "people" formally addressed their grandfather, but they seemed to know him pretty well. The company of courtroom workers seemed to enjoy each other, and they seemed to enjoy Manny. Actually, he loved it. They were serious sometimes. They were funny sometimes. They said things he didn't understand sometimes. But, because he belonged to Judge O'Connell, Manny was often the center of attention.

After lunch, Manny went back to his spot in the courtroom. He watched a few more hearings, but as he sat there, he began to reflect on what he had seen that day. Certain feelings began to rise up in Manny that he had never felt before. Years later, while filling out his application to the University of Texas Law School, he encountered an essay prompt that read:

"Tell us about the first time you felt a passion for the American legal system."

Manny responded as follows:

> I was sitting in my grandfather's courtroom at age fourteen. I had spent the whole day observing the proceedings and interacting with the people involved. The clerk and attorneys left me with the distinct impression that they cared about the American legal system. The work that they were doing mattered to them. As a young man, I began to envision myself working in this environment where everyone played different roles, but passionately pursued just outcomes for those who had so much at stake in each proceeding. The stakes were high for those who were there to right a wrong that had happened. The stakes were high for those seeking their own personal freedom. I, myself, had walked that particular path.
>
> I knew what it was like to be charged with a juvenile crime. Thankfully, the Court (and my school) granted me the opportunity to pay my debt to society without suffering jail time or expulsion. As I sat in the courtroom that day, I was thankful that I was dealt with fairly and justly, given my crime and my circumstances. Even now, I am thankful because I was able to stay in school and learn. My educa-

tional experiences in high school and college have now put me in a position to apply to your fine institution.

As I considered these things, and imagined what it might be like to work with such impassioned people working toward a noble purpose, I thought how great it could be to work specifically with kids. Kids in the system, like I was in the system. Is that possible? As I pondered that question, this strong feeling started to rise up within me. Yes! I want to work with children in the criminal justice system. I know what it's like. I know how they feel and what they're thinking!

Furthermore, the newly born passion within me was stoked as my favorite verse from the Bible came to mind. Psalm 147, verse 3 says this:

"He heals the brokenhearted

And binds up their wounds (healing their pain and comforting their sorrow)."

As a fourteen-year-old sitting in my grandfather's courtroom, drawn in to the purpose-driven working environment, I thought to myself, 'Surely if there is anywhere where people are hurting and in need of God's healing, it is here in this place.' So, in addition to the vocational passion arising within me, there was another passion born in me that day: to be used by God as an instrument of His care and concern for those who so desperately need Him. What could be better than that?

So, as a result, I set out to research the laws governing the juvenile justice system in Texas. I was able to connect what I read in the Texas Family Code and the Texas Code of Criminal Procedure with my own experience in that system as a young man.

"Now this is eternal life: that they know you, the only true God, and Jesus Christ, whom you have sent."
John 17:3

19

SAMMY LIKE JESUS

A few weeks later, Grandpa sat at a table near the window in a favorite donut shop with Sammy and Manny.

"Now boys, I want to show you one of my favorite games. I'm going to take part of this paper placemat here and fold it up like this. You see?"

The boys watched as Grandpa folded the paper into a tight triangular shape. As he sipped his coffee and took a bite of his old-fashioned donut, he flicked the triangle across the table, and so began a tutorial of paper football. The boys were delighted to thump the triangle through the air toward Grandpa's finger goalposts. They were flicking and laughing as a man approached their table. It was a fellow judge from Poplarton who stepped toward Grandpa, while extending his hand. "Judge O'Connell, how nice to see you and your grandsons enjoying donuts together."

Manny faked a cough, in the midst of it, grunting, "The people." Sammy laughed at his brother's cleverly disguised code language. However, this time it wasn't disguised enough.

Judge Spavitz looked at Manny with curiosity, raising an eyebrow. Judge O'Connell addressed his colleague, now slightly embarrassed.

"Yes, well, it seems like one grandson has developed an annoying cough."

After thirty seconds of pleasantries, Judge Spavitz got in line. Judge O'Connell sat back down. "Boys, what was that about? You embarrassed me. That's rude. Never do that again. What did you say? 'The people'? What does that mean?"

Manny said, "Grandpa, we are sorry. We have this code word for people who call you by your different names. They treat you with respect and say nice things, but don't get to know you the way Sammy and I know you. We feel special because 'the people' address you as 'sir'or 'your honor', but we are the ones who get to play paper football with you while we eat donuts."

"I see. Well, I guess that's not so bad. But, please, just wink at each other or something. No more coughs or whispering, ok?"

They both agreed and answered in unison, "Ok."

"So, that reminds me of something, actually. Manny, your parents have told me that you've been asking about the goodness of God, yes?"

Manny looked at Sammy and then back to his Grandpa. 'Yes, yes sir, I have."

"That's good! So, may I ask what's driving that question? It's a great question, Manny. I'm just curious to know more of your thoughts and feelings about God."

Manny nodded and then thought for a few moments. "My feelings are mixed up. What I really want to know is, can I trust Him? Does He love me? Is He for me?" A few more moments passed before he furrowed his brow and said, "Or is He out to get me?"

Grandpa looked across the table into Manny's face. "Thank you for being so honest. I think that's where we all begin. How we answer the questions you just asked leads us into or away from relationship with God. They're so important, Manny."

Manny nodded acknowledgment. Grandpa then continued.

"So I want you to think about something. Do you remember when you didn't like me, but you still addressed me with respect?"

"Yes."

"Well, who helped you cross the divide from 'the people' to uhm, well, playing games with me?"

"Sammy."

Sammy gave his brother a high-five.

"How? How did he do that?"

"He was just himself. You were just yourself. I watched you guys… the way you are with each other. I liked it. Eventually, I decided to join in."

Grandpa looked at Sammy. "Did Sammy ever have to convince you I was good?"

"Yeah, I mean, sometimes he would say things to me. He was really mad that day when I ran away from you. He didn't want me to think you were a monster. He knew it wasn't true, so he told me so. So yeah, he did that, but mainly I learned how to be your grandkid by watching him and watching you."

Grandpa sipped his coffee while looking at the boys intently. He said warmly, "Manny, you may have the chance to understand the gospel better than most. Do you know why?"

"Why?"

"It's really exciting to me, actually, because I think you can see this. Jesus and God have always had the Father-Son relationship with each other, right? You've read enough of John's gospel to know that Jesus really knows and loves His Father, right? And vice-versa, the Father really knows and loves Jesus?"

Manny's wheels were spinning. "Yes, I've read that."

Grandpa then nodded toward Judge Spavitz. "And the rest of us didn't enjoy their relationship, right. We were just 'the people' as you put it?"

Manny's voice rose in curiosity. "Yes, ok."

Grandpa smiled. "We were respectful but kept our distance. Nobody wanted to invite Him to dinner, right?"

Now Manny smiled. "Right."

"Well, what if the whole point of Jesus' coming was to include us in their relationship just as Sammy now includes you in our relationship?"

After a few seconds, Manny's eyes brightened with realization. "He wants us to see His Dad like He sees Him. Is that right?"

"Precisely!" beamed Grandpa.

Manny smiled. "I think I see what you're saying. Religious people call Him by the God names, but Jesus called Him 'Father'. I once called you 'Judge', but now I call you 'Grandpa'. Ha! Sammy, you're Jesus!"

Sammy was feeling the effects of a consumed apple fritter. He thrust his fist into the air. "Yes!! I'm Jesus!"

The donut eaters at the neighboring tables (which included Judge Spavitz) then glanced toward Sammy with contempt.

Feeling the attentive stares, Manny let out an agitated whisper toward his brother, "No, no, I meant you're LIKE Jesus because you let me in on your relationship with Grandpa. I can now see him as you have always seen him."

They sat quietly for almost an entire minute while Manny thought further. Thinking out loud, he then said, "Huh, so

Jesus wants to take us religious people and make us see that we are really the Father's kids like He is. That's kind of amazing."

Grandpa smiled and gave Manny space to process further. After a few seconds, Grandpa said, "You see it, don't you."

"I see it," said Manny. "I see it."

Grandpa concluded with one last statement. "As Dr. C. Baxter Kruger, a well-known author, likes to say, 'The good news of the gospel is not that we can receive Jesus Christ into our lives. The good news of the gospel is that Jesus has received us into His life and into His relationship with His Father.'"

Fifteen minutes later, Grandpa dropped the boys off at their house. They walked in the front door, finding Phil making a sandwich in the kitchen.

"Hi Dad, we're back! We're going to shoot some hoops," said Manny.

As the boys headed back toward the front door, Sammy blurted out: "Grandpa said He's God and I'm Jesus!"

Manny followed up: "Yeah! And I'm humanity!"

While dicing an onion, Phil said, "Wow, ok, cool." He thought a second longer before yelling, "Hey, wait! What? Come back here and explain yourselves!"

The boys raced back into the kitchen, and Manny explained the analogy.

"I see," said Phil. He smiled and looked at them. "You know, my memory of the Bible is that Jesus had a FATHER, not a GRANDFATHER." Phil could see Manny's face turn thoughtful.

After a moment, he said, "Yeah, you're right."

Sammy said, "Yeah, you can be God, Dad."

Phil, after an awkward pause, responded, "No, that's okay.

I can see what Grandpa is saying. It's quite profound, actually."

Phil looked at Manny. "You were scared of him and thought he was out to get you and make your life miserable." Turning to Sammy, he said, "You knew who he really was, because you knew him. You showed Manny what it was like to be loved by him, so Manny began to know him like you know him. The parallels are really, really interesting."

After a long pause, Phil smiled and said, "Now, let me show you who is God on the basketball court."

"Yeah! Dad's going to play. Let's go!" exclaimed Sammy. The father and his sons went through the back door, as it slammed behind them.

Phil's sandwich remained on the kitchen counter, only half-made.

20

PANCAKES AND LUCAS

One month later, Phil drove Manny to the boys' home on a Saturday morning. As Manny opened the passenger door, Phil spotted Mr. Phipps walking across the parking lot. He rolled down his window and said, "Mr. Phipps, good morning. I'm sorry Manny has missed the Bible study these past few weeks. We were out of town one weekend. Plus, we had some family birthday parties. He's glad to be back with you guys."

"No worries. We're glad to have him back. We should finish around 10 am or so."

"Ok, see you then."

As Manny walked toward Mr. Phipps' office, he could hear two of the boys talking. He recognized the voices before he saw who was speaking, but one of the voices was strange to his ears for a Saturday morning. Manny entered the room, matching the voices with their faces. There, across the room, sat Tommy talking to… Lucas?

Mr. Phipps abruptly walked into the room saying, "Good morning, men. I'm sorry to be late. Let's get started. Open your Bibles to Exodus, Chapter 33."

Manny sat for the next hour, astonished at Lucas's presence. He tried to pay attention to the scripture and what the other boys had to say, but it was difficult for Manny to focus. The boys' Bible study ended early. Afterward, Lucas approached Manny and whispered, "Don't look so surprised. Mr. Phipps made me come to your Jesus club. I know you, Manny. You're not any better than me, so don't look at me that way."

Manny, trying not to look surprised, looked back at Lucas. "Ok, can we be friends now?"

Lucas stared off into the distance, rubbed his chin, and said, "Come with me."

"What? Where?"

"Don't be a baby. Like I said, I know you. You like pancakes. Come on, let's go."

Lucas drove a car that wasn't really his. The orphanage had recently received an old car as a donation. Mr. Phipps reasoned that the orphanage's licensed drivers could share the car to get around town and run personal errands. At this time, Lucas was the only licensed driver in the orphanage, so he regarded the old car as his own.

Manny followed Lucas out to the car in the parking lot. "I guess you're driving now?" said Manny nervously. He then looked over his shoulder and sheepishly grinned at Mr. Phipps, who watched with a grin of his own.

Manny took a deep breath while sitting down in the car.

A few moments later, Phil's phone buzzed. He read the text, before saying to Sarah, "I just got this text from Manny. He says he's going out for pancakes with Lucas. He also says that Lucas will bring him home afterward."

"Lucas?" Sarah replied in a gasp. "That demon child from the boys' home?"

"Yeah."

"The one that made Manny's life a living hell? The one that hit you in the back?"

"Yep."

"Phil, should we go find Manny and bring him home? I don't want him to get hurt."

"I think it's ok," said Phil. "This could be good, actually. I'll track him on my phone."

Phil's phone tracker showed that Manny was now at a local diner. It took some bravery for Manny to get into Lucas' car, but now that they were at the diner, Manny was feeling more comfortable.

Manny sat across the table from Lucas, who looked at him and saying nothing. Manny said nothing back. Then Lucas blurted out:

"Mr. Phipps says I need to take all of my hatred toward you and give it over to Jesus."

Manny, not knowing what to say, said, "How does a person do that?"

Instantly, Lucas replied, "I don't know. He also says I need to take all my anger about not being adopted and... I'm sorry, but I just look over at you with your dumb face. I think, 'how could such an idiot be adopted by such great parents? How could YOU be in a family now, while I'M still stuck here with Mr. Phipps?' Anyway, he says I need to give all that over to Jesus also."

Manny absorbed the offensive insult. "Ok. That's a lot for you to deal with. Uhm, I don't know what to say. My grandpa says that..."

"I don't care what your stupid grandpa says!" Lucas erupted. "He's not your grandpa anyway. He's just the guy whose kid decided to adopt you. He had no choice but to..."

Manny, now angry, erupted back, "The good news of the gospel isn't that we can receive Jesus into our life!" Manny surprised himself with his volume and tone. A few diners were now looking over at him. He continued more calmly and quietly, "The good news of the gospel is that Jesus has received us into His life and His relationship with His Father. Do you see the difference?"

"What are you talking about? You don't know ANYTHING!"

The waiter delivered a plateful of pancakes to each of them and left.

"And neither does your so-called grandpa."

"Lucas, why am I here? I don't think I can help you like this. I can't handle the insults anymore."

"Manny, I don't WANT your help. Just eat your pancakes. You want to be friends? Eat your pancakes."

Manny did as he was told. He silently talked to Jesus, "Lord, you've accepted me into your life. Is this your life? Taking insults while eating pancakes?" Manny smiled to himself as he thought, "I guess it is."

Between bites, Lucas uttered, "I've only got one year left. By Texas law, I have one year to be adopted or get kicked out of the home. I'm sure Phipps is looking forward to that day."

Feeling helpless, Manny simply nodded and kept eating.

After a few minutes of silent pancake eating, the waiter returned to slide the bill onto the table while saying, "I'll take care of you whenever you're ready."

Lucas immediately thrust cash into the waiter's hand. He used a month's worth of his orphan allowance to pay for the entire bill.

He then looked at Manny and said, "I guess you're not so bad. Let's do this again next week?"

Manny hesitantly responded, "Yeah, ok, sure… thanks for paying for my …"

"Let's go," interrupted Lucas.

When Manny arrived home, he had a captive audience. Sarah and Phil listened attentively as Manny recounted, precisely, what was said and how it was said during the strange pancake breakfast.

While Manny was describing these events, Sammy entered the room to listen for a minute. At one point, Sammy interrupted his brother saying, "WHO did you have pancakes with?"

"Lucas."

Sammy opened his eyes wide, "The evil kid?"

"Yeah."

Sammy continued, "The one who..."

Manny, Phil, and Sarah simultaneously replied, "Yes!"

"Ok, ok," said Sammy.

Manny chuckled at his brother. He then finished describing the pancake breakfast, "Lucas insisted on paying for my breakfast before we left."

Sarah sighed aloud and furrowed her brow. "Emmanuel, I don't want you to go with him again. I don't think you can help him. You're only fifteen, and he obviously needs some serious counseling."

"Mom, as it turns out, he doesn't want me to help him. He just wants me to sit there, take his insults, while I eat pancakes! Any kid can do that."

"But, why would you WANT to do that?" said Sarah.

"I don't want to. But I want to be his friend."

When Manny returned from the diner on the following Saturday, Sarah was at home waiting for him. Daisy, the family dog, was at her knee when Manny walked through the door.

"Emmanuel, hi. Do you know if Daisy got her stomach pill this morning? She's really gassy today."

"Hi Mom. I think Dad forgot. I didn't give it to her, no. It's gross."

"Ok, I'll do it. How did it go with Lucas?"

Manny's shoulders slumped. "Mom, I think you're right. I

can't handle these pancakes. I was dumb and asked him about his birth parents. He told me that he doesn't know anything about them… nothing at all. He doesn't even know their names. It's really sad, but then he got really nasty. He took it all out on me… lots of, uhm, rage. He said he hates me again."

Sarah swooped in to hug her son, and he buried his face into her shoulder. "I can't handle it, Mom. I can't handle it. He's too hard."

Sarah, now feeling sympathy for both of the pancake boys, squeezed her boy and teared up. "You are loved, sweetie. You are loved so, so much." She released to look Manny in the face. "You know that, right? I don't tell you that enough. And, uhm, and I am so, so proud of you and your pursuit of Lucas. You encourage my faith. You make me believe all the more that Jesus is alive and living in my boy. Look at the way he's loving the unlovable."

Manny plopped down on the couch, and Sarah sat near him. She said, "Hey, I have an idea. Listen to me. I actually know how to make pancakes myself." She smiled. Manny smiled back.

"What if, next Saturday, you guys don't go to the diner. In fact, at this point, I never want you to go to that diner again." Sarah smiled. Manny smiled back.

She continued. "What if, instead, you came here? I could make you guys some pancakes!"

Manny was quiet for a moment and then said, "Will you guys sit at the table with us?"

Perceiving why her son would make such a request, Sarah teared up again. "It must have been really bad today, Manny. Yes, of course, it's about time we stepped in to support you. We won't leave your side. I promise."

On the following Tuesday, Lucas's conscience was bothering him about how he had treated Manny on Saturday. He paced the inner yard of the boys' home, lost in his thoughts. Even he knew that his inner turmoil and confusion caused him to lash out at Manny. But why would Manny take the lashing? He thought to himself, "Why would he take my abuse like that? No pancake is worth that."

Once again feeling terrible about his own behavior but powerless to change it, Lucas marched into Mr. Phipps' office.

Mr. Phipps looked up from his messy desk and saw Lucas. "Hi Lucas, I don't have time to..."

Lucas sat down in a chair and said, "Mr. Phipps, we need to talk."

Mr. Phipps sighed aloud and said, "Ok, Lucas, what is it?"

Hardly waiting for Mr. Phipps to finish the sentence, Lucas said, "I'm not coming to the Bible club anymore. I've tried Jesus out for a while. He's not doing me any good. I'm sorry, but you can't make me go. Not anymore."

Mr. Phipps sighed again and said, "You're right, Lucas. I can't make you, but I'm sorry you feel that way. I thought you liked getting time with Manny afterward. How was that going? Did something happen?"

"Yeah, something happened. I found out I didn't like him that much."

In a moment of clarity, Mr. Phipps asked, "Maybe you found out that you don't like YOU that much?" These words penetrated deep. Somehow, they got past all of Lucas' defenses, piercing his soul. Mr. Phipps could see on Lucas' face that he was conflicted. He wanted to deny such a stupid notion and quickly leave the office with a scoff, but he also wanted to acknowledge his own self-hatred and seek refuge in Mr. Phipps. To Mr. Phipps' eye, it really looked like Lucas might burst. At last, Mr. Phipps said, "Lucas, you are loved."

Now, the Lucas dam burst. "Ha, what a laugh! By who? I have nobody in this world. Nobody! Ha! Nobody LIKES me, how could they LOVE me? You know who dislikes me the most? ME! I CAN'T STAND ME! I'm living in hell because I have to live with myself! There's no way out, Mr. Phipps. I have no way out of this life. I'm so disgusting. I buy Manny pancakes so I can use him for target practice. Why would I do that? I hate myself for doing that, but he just sits there and takes it. Why would he do that? He must know that it makes me despise myself even more."

Mr. Phipps roared back, "He does it because he wants to be your friend."

"Why? I've heaped nothing but abuse on that poor boy his entire life. I'm older than him. I should have looked out for him all these years, but instead I heaped upon him abuse after abuse. Why would he want to be my friend? Tell me!"

In a calm, simple tone, Mr. Phipps said plainly, "Jesus lives in Manny. Jesus is pursuing you through Manny."

At that moment, Lucas' phone lit up with a text message notification. The text message was from Manny. It read:

"Hey Lucas, my mom wants to make us pancakes on Saturday. Do you want to come over after Bible study?"

Mr. Phipps saw that Lucas had become distracted by his phone and said, "What is it?"

Lucas' body went limp, falling back into the chair. "It's Manny. He wants to know if I can come over on Saturday for pancakes."

Mr. Phipps smiled a knowing smile. Lucas, still contemplating the text message, got up from the chair. He quietly walked toward the door. "I'll see you later, Mr. Phipps."

"Ok. I'll see you later, Lucas."

On Saturday morning, Manny walked into the kitchen to greet Sarah, who was reaching for the griddle in a high cabinet.

"Mom, I'll get it for you." He grabbed the griddle and set it on the counter. "Mom, Lucas never answered my text messages. I really don't think he's coming over later."

"Oh, I'm sorry to hear that. How disappointing!" She thought a moment while looking at the griddle. "Well, I've got a griddle and the ingredients for batter, so I guess you will still have pancakes when you get back."

She smiled and kissed his cheek as a farewell.

"Ok, thanks Mom! Oh! I gave Daisy her stomach pill just now. I put it in her food. I'll see you later."

"Thanks, sweetheart, for doing that. I'm not so sure about those pills. She seems to be getting worse with the gas. Poor thing." Manny said goodbye to his mom as Phil summoned him toward the car.

A few minutes later, Phil parked in the parking lot of the boys' home, as Manny looked around for Lucas' car. He told Phil that he didn't see it, so Phil could tell Sarah for certain that Lucas would not be coming over.

Manny walked inside and sat down. Mr. Phipps walked by, squeezing Manny's shoulder as he continued to walk by him. Manny looked up at Mr. Phipps as he sat down in a chair. They gave each other knowing looks as if to say, "Yeah, it's sad that he's not here."

Phil picked Manny up after the Bible study and brought him home. As they pulled into the driveway, Manny saw his grandparents' car parked on the street.

"Are Grandpa and Wemaw here?"

Phil enthusiastically replied, "Yeah! Mom invited them over. She thought that might cheer you up."

"Awesome!"

Manny walked into the house and warmly greeted his grandparents. The aroma in the kitchen was heavenly. He then saw the golden brown, perfectly formed round cakes stacked high on a plate.

"Well, are we ready?" said Sarah. "I hope these are as good

as your diner, Emmanuel," she said with a smile.

"I can't wait, Mom!"

"Me neither!" said Sammy.

They sat down at the table, as Phil said, "Grandpa, would you bless the food?"

Grandpa said, "Sure!" and was just about to ask the blessing when the doorbell rang.

The family members looked across the table at each other in wonder. Who could that be? Phil said, "Manny, maybe you should go to the door?"

Manny opened the door to find Lucas staring at him.

"I was hungry for some pancakes." He grinned. "I thought I might find some here."

Manny, trying not to look surprised, said, "Yeah, we've got pancakes, come on in."

Lucas walked inside, saw the family gathered around the table, and thought. "What am I doing here?"

He whispered to Manny, "Hey man, I didn't realize..."

Just then, Lucas felt a tug on his pant leg as the family dog was nestling in to be petted. Simultaneously, Sarah came over to introduce herself.

"Hi, Lucas, I'm Mrs. Marshall. Manny's mom." She extended her hand.

Lucas shook it and then gave Daisy a pet on the back. "Manny, look at how Daisy is greeting your friend. Lucas, she never pays attention to strangers."

He petted her again. "Good dog."

Lucas approached the table, as Sarah introduced everyone by name. It was a little awkward for Phil because of the back beating, but they all managed to look Lucas in the eye and warmly greet him.

Sarah invited Lucas to sit down at the table between her and Manny. She pointed toward the empty chair, saying, "Manny's Grandpa was just about to offer thanks for our meal." Lucas' racing pulse was felt by Sarah and Manny as they held his hand during the prayer. The room was silent until Grandpa began with "Dear Heavenly Father…"

As Grandpa took a breath, the room was filled with a thunderous eruption of gas. Daisy had let loose with an unusually long-lasting noxious explosion that went on for three seconds, at least. She was lying on the ground approximately five feet from the table. She placed one of her front paws over her face and let out a slight whimper. Grandpa was stunned and could not continue. Manny's bowed head looked up at Sammy, who burst into laughter. Manny started laughing also. In fact, a moment later, every person at the table, including Lucas, was laughing heartily. Phil ran over to Daisy and said, "Poor Daisy, she can't help it," as he patted her head. "Go ahead, Grandpa," he instructed.

"Loving Father, thank you for this gathering. Would You bless this food and bless our time together? We pray that You would pour out Your compassion on this dog, Daisy. She is one of your creatures, so we pray for her relief. In Jesus' name. Amen."

Everyone giggled a little, smiled, and at once said, "Amen."

21

SEEKING AND FINDING

The next day, Lucas schemed a new scheme. He waited for his roommates to leave their shared bedroom, so he could be alone. His plan was to sit in the silence to think about the day before. As the last roommate left for the day, Lucas pulled out a chair. He then sat down in the center of the room between the bunk beds on each side. He sat, and he remembered. He tried to feel what it felt like to be at that table surrounded by those people. He became entranced thinking about each face. He thought about the things they said to him. He thought about the questions they asked him. He tried to summon once again the feeling of belonging he felt at that table.

One of the roommates forgot his lunch and returned to the room. The roommate saw Lucas entranced. Lucas never heard him rummage through his things or pick up his crinkly lunch bag. Lucas never heard the roommate say to a neighboring orphan in the hallway, "Lucas is in there. I think he's high." No, Lucas was thinking about Daisy, laughter, pancakes, and the warmth of being surrounded by family.

Then, at that moment, the warm memories ceased as he began to think, "But, they're not my family, are they?"

Suddenly, Lucas remembered a scripture framed that hung on the wall of the boys' home commons. He had seen the scripture a hundred times, but never actually considered it before now. In his mind's eye, it read:

> *"A Father to the fatherless, a defender of widows, is*
> *God in his holy dwelling,*
> *God sets the lonely in families, he leads out the prisoners with singing."*
> Psalm 68:5-6

Lucas's mood shifted from joy to bitterness. He suddenly resented Mr. Phipps (or whoever it was) who posted this scripture. If this scripture was from the Bible, he suddenly despised the Bible.

Was Lucas not lonely? "I've never been set in a family," he thought. "Never! I never will!" His emotions were fueled by the previous day's experience of love and belonging. Never experiencing that beauty before meant that he never knew what he was missing. Now, he knew what it might be like. This experience produced a longing in his heart. This longing made the impossibility of family seem cruel. Consequently, the scriptural promise seemed laughable.

Now irritated, Lucas found himself saying words that surprised him. He genuinely surprised himself by saying aloud:

"God, if You're here..."

"No!" he thought. "I'm not doing that..." But he couldn't help himself and continued.

"I'm sure You're not here... I'm not sure You exist, and if You do, why would You be here ... But, if You are, You must see how cruel the scripture words must seem to me...I've never been set in a family. You never did that for me. Why? Until yesterday, I never knew what a family might be like. And, why does Manny get to be in a family, and I don't? You really aren't here, are You? I'm sure You wouldn't like being accused by me. If You hate me, that's fine, but don't taunt me with love. That's too much for a person to feel. It's mean and dirty behavior that's beneath a god, don't You think? You must have better things to do than taunt me. Leave me alone."

This last sentence to God made Lucas confused. "Why did I say that? I don't really want to be alone, do I? I'm so confused… better end the prayer now."

"Amen, or whatever. I need to drive."

Suddenly, Lucas got up, pushed the chair in, and walked to the parking lot. When he sat down in his car, he suddenly felt the way he felt the last time he was in his car. On the way back after pancakes, he felt liked and included. There they were again. As he drove, he thought about the mom, the dad, the old Memaw or Remaw, the grandpa, and the boys. They all filled his mind and imagination. Suddenly, the boys were no longer imaginary… there they were! Without thinking, Lucas had driven back toward the Marshall's house. Now he was on their street. The boys were outside playing basketball in the driveway.

"Embarrassing!" he thought. "They're waving me down."

"Isn't that Lucas?" said Sammy.

"Yeah! I wonder if he plays basketball? Hey! Hey Lucas! Wait!!"

Lucas stopped the car in the middle of the street while rolling down his window.

Manny said, "Hey! Do you want to play basketball with us?"

"Ok," said Lucas. He parked the car on the curb.

After Lucas, Manny, and Sammy played for several

minutes, Phil joined them. They played basketball together for another twenty minutes. Afterward, Phil went inside to take a water break. While Phil was inside, another car pulled up and parked on the curb. Grandpa dropped off Sarah as he said to her, "When will your car be ready for pick up? I can take you back to the mechanic when it's ready."

"Tomorrow. Thanks! Do you want to come inside for a minute, Dad?"

"I can't believe my eyes," replied Grandpa. He exited the driver's door, suddenly motivated to walk with Sarah toward the house.

"Hi boys! Hi Lucas, it's nice to see you again," Sarah said. The boys stopped playing momentarily to greet the adults. Grandpa approached as he made eye contact with Lucas.

"Lucas, I never had the chance to ask you yesterday, but what have you thought about all the Jesus talk on Saturday mornings?"

Lucas's eye was suddenly drawn to the family dog lying in the yard behind Grandpa.

"Hmm, well, how is Daisy doing?"

Grandpa, with a confused look on his face, said, "I'm sorry?"

Lucas snapped, "Daisy, that's the dog's name, right? When you prayed for that animal yesterday, was that real or just for show?"

Grandpa gave a pained expression as Lucas inwardly thought, "Whoa, you idiot! Why do I say such things? No wonder people don't like me."

Sarah interjected, "We are still trying to figure her out, Lucas. But thank you for your concern for her. She really likes you too."

Grandpa smiled and said, "Lucas, I can see you're a practical kinda guy. I like that. I must confess I had forgotten about praying for her. But my feelings were sincere at the time."

Manny and Sammy withdrew from the awkward conversation and to renew their hoop shooting. Sarah went inside.

Lucas looked down at the ground and said to Grandpa, "Manny says you think Jesus accepts us into His life and not the other way around… I've always heard it's the other way around… So, I might be interested in talking about that sometime."

Grandpa smiled broadly and said, "I'd like that. Maybe you, Manny and I could get lunch together sometime and talk?"

Sammy overheard this invitation, then interjected, "And me too. Don't forget… I'm Jesus!"

Lucas gave Sammy a curious side-eyed glance.

"Ok, sounds good," he said back to Grandpa.

Grandpa extended his hand toward Lucas, shook it, walked back toward his car and drove away.

As Sarah entered the house, she suddenly saw Phil. "I didn't know you were home. HI!" She greeted him with a kiss.

"Hi there, I guess you saw Lucas?"

"Yes, I left him talking with Dad."

Phil said, "As strange as it may sound given our history, I kind of like that kid." Phil's words trailed off as he stared into space.

Sarah said, "Sweetie. Hey, where did you go? Phil, don't go getting any ideas, ok? We can't adopt the entire boys' home."

"No, I know. It's just that I could tell he was enjoying the pancakes and family time yesterday. I guess he hasn't experienced much of that in his life." He paused, then continued. "I think it's interesting that he came back over today, that's all."

"It is interesting. Maybe now he can spend time with Manny without saying hateful things to him."

Phil's eyes met his wife's gaze. "Yes, I hope so too."

On the following Saturday afternoon, Lucas was sitting at a table in the familiar diner. He watched as Grandpa and Manny entered and walked toward him. He greeted them with a question.

"Where's Jesus?"

Grandpa smiled broadly. "He has a soccer game."

After ordering coffee and pancakes, Grandpa looked at Lucas while saying, "So, a dear friend would always say to me, 'The good news of the gospel isn't that we can accept Jesus into our lives…'"

Lucas interrupted. "No, wait. I don't want to talk about that today."

Manny and Grandpa looked at each other.

Lucas continued, "No, there's something else. Why would the Bible say that God sets the lonely in families? He's never done that for me. What's that about?"

Grandpa thought a moment. "Actually, that verse begins by saying that God is a 'Father to the Fatherless', so really, it begins with you and Him. I guess He reasons that if you don't like Him, you won't like His family very much."

"Me and Him, huh? Well, I DON'T like Him. Why should I?"

"Can I say something?" said Manny.

"No!" said Lucas.

"Listen to him, Lucas. He's been where you are," said Grandpa.

Manny continued, "I didn't think I liked Him either. But I've changed my mind. He is what you're looking for. He is light. He is truth, and He is love."

"Whatever."

Grandpa calmly looked into Lucas' face. "Lucas, look at

me. You can see that He's coming after you, can't you. 'A Father to the Fatherless', you think it's too good to be true in your case, so you resist. But you know He loves you, don't you? You can feel His heart in me, and Manny's mom, and Manny. Why would Manny sit with you while taking your abuse? You know why! Mr. Phipps has taught you enough about Jesus to recognize Him when He's right in front of you. Right? Yeah, you can see that He's coming after you in His love for you. Stop resisting, Lucas! Give in to it and rest in His love for you. He won't leave you holding an empty bag. Lucas, there's nothing like being loved by Him."

Lucas was now visibly softening. His face relaxed. He looked over at Manny, who was nodding along with Grandpa. He looked back at Grandpa and said in a soft, low voice, "Could you pray for me? I don't know how to be anything other than what I am. I can't escape."

Without hesitation, Grandpa began, "Loving Father, I lift up our friend Lucas here into Your loving arms. We pray that Your light would swallow up the darkness and penetrate Lucas' heart deep, deep down. I believe he wants You, but doesn't yet know how to receive Your love for him. Dear Lord, envelop him that he might actually feel Your embrace and take hold of Your life-changing Fatherhood. Be true. Be real. Be here with us now as Manny and I need You too. For Your name's sake. Amen."

Manny looked up just in time to hear Lucas say, "Excuse me." Lucas began walking toward the door of the diner. When he reached the door, he began to run. The waiter looked back toward the table still occupied by Manny and Grandpa.

Manny said, "Should I run after him?"

"No, let him go. What he needs to do, he doesn't want you to see."

Grandpa was right. Lucas entered his car, so he could let

it all go. His emotions burst forth as he allowed himself to feel and welcome God into his heart of hearts. Between sobs, he only said one word, "Ok." In a voice of acknowledgment and surrender, over and over again, Lucas said, "Ok."

After a few minutes of intense release and acceptance, Lucas composed himself, so that he could pray. "God, lead me into Your truth. Who are You exactly? Teach me who You are and who I am to You. You are a father to the fatherless. I am fatherless, so I take You as my Father. I put down all my defenses in Your presence ... You can love me ... I won't fight You. Please don't leave me alone."

He took deep breaths and, in between breaths, said, "Whew, ok. Ok. Ok. I am Yours. Ok."

A few minutes later, Manny's phone displayed a new text message from Lucas:

"Please tell your Grandpa that I'm sorry for leaving. But God is good. I'm His now, and He is mine. If it's ok, I'd like to see you both again very soon."

Manny said, "Hey, Grandpa, look."

Grandpa read the text, and grabbed his grandson's shoulder. A tear escaped his eye as he said, "Praise the Lord, Manny. Let's be sure to keep praying for him. Ok?"

Manny sniffled. "Yeah. Ok."

Over the next several weeks, Lucas spent extended time with Mr. Phipps after the boys' Bible study each Saturday. Lucas was like a sponge soaking up as much as Mr. Phipps could teach him about Jesus and Jesus' Father. In addition, Grandpa asked Lucas to come over and help him with different home maintenance projects around his house. They often discussed the gospel while painting a fence, cleaning gutters, or washing cars.

On one such occasion, Lucas walked into the house to grab a bottle of water for Grandpa and for himself. As he entered the house, the old grandfather clock indicated that it was 11 am with its loud, haunting gongs. As Lucas reached into the refrigerator, Wemaw entered the kitchen. Lucas had met this lady and seen her come and go as he worked with Grandpa, but they had only exchanged pleasantries. She seemed nice enough, but Lucas couldn't help but feel a little afraid of the woman.

As he reached into the refrigerator, the eleventh dong was still hanging in the air as Wemaw said to him in a commanding tone, "Young man."

Lucas shuddered but then replied, "Yes ma'am?"

Her voice softened. She said to him, "Can I give you a hug? Sometimes, you look to me like you need a hug."

"Yes ma'am."

She hugged him warmly in a hug where Lucas started out rigid, but melted after a second or two. Afterward, she patted him on the arm and said, "Don't let him work you too hard."

And, then she went back upstairs.

A FEW WEEKS LATER, Manny was sitting on the pew on a Sunday morning. For some reason, Manny's mood was sour. He had snagged a slight hole in his dress shirt, and none of the worship songs had been to his liking. Once again, Manny found himself sitting between his grandparents, occasionally distracted by the activities of the other family members. During the sermon, he heard the slight rustling of the mint ritual. He looked over as his mother slyly placed the mint from her hand into Sammy's open hand. He was sitting on her right. Then something unusual happened. The rustling continued as she pulled out another mint and slyly offered it to Lucas sitting on her left. This irked Manny. "I never get a mint," he thought. "She gave one to Lucas. I can't believe it."

After the sermon ended and the final worship song was

sung, Manny watched as his friend with fresh breath went forward to the front of the church. Soon after, it was announced by the pastor that Lucas had expressed a desire to be baptized. Furthermore, the pastor explained that instead of him doing the honors, another person named Henry Phipps would receive Lucas' confession of faith and baptize him in the name of the Father, the Son, and the Holy Spirit. It was unusual to be sure, but the pastor explained that Mr. Phipps' involvement was entirely appropriate under the circumstances.

Several minutes later, Mr. Phipps entered the baptistry with Lucas. He asked him if he believed that Jesus was the son of God who had lived and died for the forgiveness of his sins and was raised from the dead three days later. Lucas heartily said, "I do!" and Mr. Phipps took him under the water and raised him back up out of the water. The congregation cheered as Phil smiled and looked over at his wife.

Sarah, with tears streaming down her cheeks, said, "Don't look at me like that, Phil. We can't adopt the entire boys' home." Phil laughed while looking back at Lucas standing in the baptistry.

After church, Grandpa and Wemaw hosted a celebratory luncheon for Lucas. Mr. and Mrs. Phipps joined the Marshalls around the O'Connell's table. Lucas smiled, and laughed, and beamed. While passing meat loaf, Wemaw whispered to Sarah, "He seems so happy." Happy Lucas was given a tour of the house by Sammy, but Manny kept his distance. Sammy took Lucas to "the upstairs." When they arrived back down at the base of the stairs, the grandfather clock struck 3 pm loudly. Lucas reacted with a grimace.

"So, do you think it's my imagination?" asked Sammy.

"No. You're right. It's definitely creepy."

When this happy luncheon was over, Lucas said his good-byes and gave hugs. He drove back to the boys' home while the Marshalls drove home. When they arrived home, the boys scattered, but Phil and Sarah talked in the front yard.

Sarah said to Phil, "It doesn't seem right for him to go back to the orphanage on a day like today. He should be with family."

Phil gave Sarah a smirky smile. She smiled back saying, "Do you think we should tell the Lord we are open to His will?"

"Yes. Let's seek His face about adopting Lucas. Just like with Manny, let's tell the Lord that we're open to hearing His voice. It's a big decision, Sarah."

She nodded and sat silently.

Phil's face shifted, becoming more serious. "Let's go before Him tonight and pray together. Ok?"

"Ok."

22

NO AND YES

On that night, the couple drew near to each other and then drew near to their God. They prayed in their room with the door closed while Sammy and Manny watched a movie in the living room. The Lord touched their hearts in the midst of their united prayer. After about 45 minutes, Phil opened the bedroom door, walked down the hall, and said with a smile, "Hey boys, is that movie any good?"

Sarah sat on the bed a bit longer. She felt the need, after this time with her heavenly Father, to call and talk with her earthly father. It was a frequent feeling. She loved her dad and constantly sought his counsel, but at the moment, she felt this need more strongly and more urgently than usual.

She called, but no one answered. Phil walked back into the bedroom saying, "Hi, do we need to pray some more?"

"No. No, it's just I feel a strong urge to talk with Dad."

After a restless night's sleep, she called Grandpa's house.

"Hi Dad, good morning."

"Good morning! I just saw that you called last night. Is everything alright?"

"Yeah, yeah, everything is fine. Phil and I just want you and Mom to know that we are praying about adopting Lucas. The idea started with Phil, actually. I kept telling him that we can't adopt the entire boys' home, but we got together last night. Uh, well, we asked the Lord to guide our family into His will for Lucas. So, anyway, I thought you and Mom might like to know and pray with us."

There was a long pause of silence that Sarah suddenly found uncomfortable. At last Grandpa said, "I see."

"Dad, what's wrong? I thought you would be overjoyed."

"It's a big decision, Sarah." His tone then brightened just a little. He then said, "Thank you for letting us know. We definitely want to be with you and Phil as you walk through the process."

"Ok, good!" she replied hopefully.

Grandpa's tone became more serious again.

"Sarah, you guys might need to hurry. Lucas told me he turns eighteen in just a few months. And, you realize that adopting an 'almost adult' won't have much legal effect. He may agree to change his name, but he may not. Also, under Texas law, once he turns eighteen, he will be making his own decisions whether he's adopted or not."

"Yes, I see. I need to know these things. Thank you! I had such a strong urge to talk to you about it all. Can you think of anything else I should know?"

He was silent for several seconds, but then spoke. "No. I think you're fully informed now." After a few more seconds of silence, he said, "We love you and are with you."

"Thanks Dad, and give Mom a hug for me."

After Grandpa said goodbye to his daughter, he set the phone down as he looked over at Wemaw. She had been near the phone, so she heard the entire conversation. Presently, she walked away and slumped her shoulders. Grandpa went over to her and hugged his wife. "It's going to be okay, sweetie. The Lord will work it out. Don't worry."

On the following Wednesday, Sarah found herself in Mr. Phipps' office. After the talk with her Dad, she and Phil felt free to take a step of inquiry into the process with Mr. Phipps. He explained to Sarah that there were certain difficulties in adopting someone as old as Lucas, but those difficulties could be overcome. Mr. Phipps had a hopeful tone, but seemed a tad cautious.

"Mrs. Marshall, uhm, Sarah, he's seventeen. The law puts certain hurdles in place to protect soon-to-be adults. They can be vulnerable to manipulation. But here's the thing: if he truly wants to be part of your family, there's no problem. When the judge asks him if his decision is voluntary, freely given, and given without coercion, he will just say 'yes', and that will be that."

"Mr. Phipps, uhm, Henry, if I may, I fully understand you. Thanks for taking the time with me this morning. You are a gift to our family. I'll be in touch, ok?"

"Ok."

Sarah closed the office door behind her. She turned to walked down the hall toward the parking lot. She was lost in thought until she looked up. Suddenly there stood Lucas in the hallway. Sarah did not want to give him false hope, so she panicked:

"Lucas, hi!" She reached over and gave him a hug. "Emmanuel's paperwork never seems to end!" she said awkwardly as she let out a sigh of fake exasperation.

Lucas looked at her strangely. "Ok, well, have a good day. Actually, I wanted you to know that I've been reading this book Mr. Phipps gave me..."

"Oh! Sorry, Lucas!" she interrupted him. "I've got to get back to the clinic. Let's talk later!"

"Ok," he said as the exit door shut behind her.

Lucas couldn't help but feel slightly let down. He hadn't heard from the family since he left their house on Sunday. He stifled his desire to belong to them somehow. He said to God under his breath, "I guess it's still just You and me. Just You and me. That's ok with me. How about You?"

Later that evening, Sarah arrived home. She told Phil about her cautiously optimistic meeting with Mr. Phipps and awkward interaction with Lucas.

Phil contemplated her words for a moment, then said, "You know, if we want to adopt him, we will need to tell him that at some point."

"I know. That just didn't seem like the time. Since we prayed, I have felt like a flat tire. We have neglected Lucas the past few days. Now, I've kinda lied to him. This week has felt clunky and strange. I don't get it."

Phil replied in an upbeat tone, "I see what you mean, dear. Things will smooth out if this is what the Lord wants. It's early days yet."

On the following morning, Phil was getting ready for work when Manny walked into the bedroom. Phil looked at him, noticing that Manny seemed weighed down.

"Hey Manny, you seem sad. Can I help?"

Manny looked down at his own feet. "Yeah, Dad, I need to tell you something."

"Lay it on me, son."

"Dad, ever since Sunday, I've felt bad about myself. I saw Mom put a mint in Lucas's hand, and, well, it made me mad. It was a great day for him. I know that. I should've been happy for him, but all I could think about was the mint."

"The mint?"

As Manny tried to explain, Phil covered his own face in shaving cream and began to shave.

"Yeah, every Sunday, Mom gives Sammy a mint, and I'm fine with that. He's her boy, and I sit way down the pew away from her, so she can't reach me. I get that. But, when I saw her give one to Lucas, I guess I got jealous."

"I see," said Phil. He stopped shaving and listened.

"I thought that feeling might go away, but after the baptism, I kept my distance from Lucas. I don't want to be like that, Dad. I was reading my Bible this morning, and it says in Ephesians that I should get rid of all bitterness, rage, and anger. And I can't, Dad. I just can't."

Phil's heart swelled with empathy toward his boy. With half his face still covered in shaving cream, he said to Manny.

"Hey, thank you for sharing that with me." He looked at Manny until Manny's eyes met his. "Hey, I mean it. Thank you. That's something we all struggle with, I promise you. Don't forget to talk to Jesus about these things. Remember, God's not out to get you. Tell Him you need Him, Manny. Actually, can I pray for you right now?"

"Can you finish shaving first?"

Phil smiled as he looked in the mirror. He complied with his son's request. He then prayed with his hand on Manny's shoulder. Manny patted his dad's arm as he said, "Amen."

"Thanks Dad. I feel better."

"Manny, please come to me. I want to be here for you, ok?"

"Ok."

When Sarah got home later that night, Phil told her every detail of this conversation. In response, Sarah freaked out.

"I'm a terrible mother! He could already feel my affections shifting toward Lucas. Of course, he was angry. He's my son. Phil, I've got to make it up to him. We have two boys. We shouldn't be chasing another one! Do I believe the Lord loves Lucas? Yes, I do, and it's been such a rich blessing to be a part of his life and transformation."

"But," Phil interjected, "we have two boys. Let's love them

well. I agree. Lucas deserves to be adopted, but I don't think it's supposed to be us."

"Right."

Phil continued. "I see that now. If I'm honest, the Lord has been speaking to my heart for a few days now. Our family is complete, and we can release Lucas into God's sovereign care." He paused a moment, squeezed his wife's hand. He then continued. "I think we have our answer. Let's tell the boys."

Sarah catapulted out of her chair in the master bedroom and ran into the living room. Sammy and Manny were shooting Nerf basketball hoops in Manny's room when they heard a loud booming male voice. "Hear ye, hear ye! All persons shall gather together for a family meeting in the living room!"

"Dad?" said Manny.

"Boys, boys, come in here, please! Right now, let's go!"

The boys ran into the room and plopped down on the couch next to their mom. Phil stood a few feet in front of them, blew his mouth trumpet proclaiming,

"Let it be known that the Marshall family meeting has come to order!"

Sammy looked at the others. "Dad's talking funny." Phil continued.

"Is there anyone among us who has business to speak before the assembly?"

Sarah raised her hand.

"Oh yes, Madame. The nice lady with the pretty smile. Mrs. Marshall, is it?"

Sammy put up his hand in protest and ran toward his dad. He whispered something into Phil's ear.

"Oh! I stand corrected. The chair recognizes DOCTOR Marshall at this time."

Sammy gave an approving nod. Manny laughed.

Sarah cleared her throat. "Thank you, Mr. Chairman. There are two things I'd like to discuss as a family. First! Your Dad and I have been praying this week about adopting Lucas into our family."

Manny's eyes grew wide. Sammy's eyes grew wider.

"BUT, we have come to believe that is NOT the Lord's will for our family, and so we will not be doing that."

Sarah saw Phil look at her curiously. Then he said with a smile, "Actually, I don't know WHY we just told you any of that. It was my idea, but I guess that wasn't necessary for you to know, but there ya go."

Manny smiled. Sammy looked confused. Sarah spoke.

"The NEXT thing on the family agenda is this: I have grown DISSATISFIED with our family seating lineup on Sunday mornings. Manny, I know you like your grandparents, but I'm going to insist that you stop sitting between them. Instead, I want you to sit next to me! I'm sorry if that's a disappointment to you, BUT I want to sit between my two boys at church!"

Manny looked at Phil, who gave him a wink. Manny then heard Sammy whisper in his ear, "Maybe you'll get a mint now!"

Phil then gave another fake trumpet blast and said, "This concludes the family meeting for tonight unless there are any other announcements!"

Sammy raised his hand. "Oh! Oh! I've got one!"

"Yes sir, you there in the red t-shirt!"

Sammy, now seeing that all eyes were on him, said, "I have a soccer game on Saturday!"

"Yes, yes, the family is aware of this. Any more announcements?"

The boys looked at each other.

"Hearing none. The family meeting is now adjourned," said Phil. "The hugs may now commence!"

Manny ran into his mother's arms. "I love you sweetie, you are my boy, ok?"

"Ok, Mom. You are my mom."

On Saturday morning, Phil took Manny to Mr. Phipps' Bible study, and Sarah took Sammy over to her parents' house.

They arrived at the door and greeted the grandparents. Wemaw took Sammy with her, while Sarah sat down in the living room with her dad.

"So? What do you hear from the Lord regarding Lucas?"

"Dad, I will say the same thing to Mom in a minute, but we really thank you for praying that we would hear the Lord clearly regarding Lucas. I think we have."

"Oh?"

"Yes, I feel a little strange because Lucas has become part of our lives. Uhm, well, we would love it if he had a family of his own, but don't believe it's supposed to be ours."

"Well, I think you're wrong there."

"No, really Dad. Phil and I feel like the Lord is saying…"

Grandpa interrupted, "Sweetheart, you misunderstand me. I believe you when you say that the Lord said 'no' about Lucas."

"You do?"

"Yes. And I think I know why."

"You do?"

"Yes, let's get Wemaw in here. Oh, Wemaw, can you bring Sammy in here, please?"

She soon arrived with Sammy close behind.

Grandpa looked at Wemaw and then said, "Sarah just told me that the Lord is not leading them to adopt Lucas." Wemaw's eyes went from questioning to hopeful.

Sammy said loudly, "Yeah, we're not getting a new brother."

Grandpa said with a smile and a twinkle in his eye, "Yes, but you may be getting a new uncle."

Sammy erupted, "Yahoo, a new uncle! Wait, what's a new uncle?"

Sarah looked at her dad amazed. "Dad, what are you saying?"

"When you called last week, we didn't answer because your mother and I were deep in prayer together, asking the Lord whether or not we should adopt Lucas. When you called the next morning to say that you and Phil were considering the same, we didn't know how to respond. I'm sorry."

"Dad, that is incredible! How self-important I must have seemed... I feel terrible."

"No, don't. We both have our answer now, so that is what is important." Wemaw hugged him tightly as he said these words.

"Ha, so I'm getting a new brother," said Sarah delightedly. "That's crazy."

"Yeah, Mom... that's crazy!" said Sammy. He looked off into space and said, "Uncle Lucas. Uncle Lucas. Yeah, I like the sound of that." Grandpa tussled his hair as the whole room laughed with him.

23

LUCAS O'CONNELL

Grandpa and Wemaw quickly said their goodbyes to Sarah and Sammy and then raced over to the boys' home. Earlier that morning, Manny had arrived at Mr. Phipps' office for Bible study. He looked across the room for Lucas. After spotting him, Manny rushed over to extend his hand. "Hey, I never said congratulations on your baptism."

Lucas shook Manny's hand. "Thanks. I haven't seen you guys this week. Well, I saw your mom, but…"

"Pancakes later? My dad gave me money, so I could pay this time."

"Sure."

"Ok, see you afterward," said Manny with a smile.

After the Bible study, Manny and Lucas were in the parking lot walking toward the car when they saw something strange.

"Hey Manny, isn't that your grandpa's car headed this way?"

Grandpa's car then rolled up next to them. Grandpa said,

"Hey, you guys. You're not going for pancakes today. Manny, I've called your dad, so he will be here soon to pick you up."

Manny and Lucas gave each other a confused look.

"Hey Lucas, is there somewhere here where the three of us could talk?" Lucas looked past Grandpa into the car, spying Wemaw sitting in the passenger seat.

"Uhm, yes, I know a spot outside in the courtyard."

"Great! Manny, there's your dad's car now. He will explain everything to you."

Manny got in the car with Phil, while the Grandparents followed Lucas to the secluded spot in the courtyard. They sat down at a picnic table. Grandpa looked at Lucas, opened his mouth to speak, but it was Wemaw's voice that came out. She knew exactly what she wanted to say, so she said it.

"Lucas, we want to apologize. You had quite a life-changing event last Sunday, but I'm afraid you didn't get much support from us this week."

"Yes ma'am, but that's..."

"Hush now. Let me finish. There was some confusion in our family, but that's all been settled now. And, well, if it's ok with you, we don't want to leave you alone ever again."

"If it's alright with me?" Lucas was touched by her words, but didn't fully understand them.

"Yes," she said. "When a person is adopted, they have to give their consent for the adoption, you see," she said, bright-faced and smiling.

"You want to adopt me?" Lucas smiled at her, but still looked baffled.

"Well, not just me." She looked at her husband.

Grandpa then spoke. "Lucas, I've cherished our time together. You know, working together at our house, and talking about Jesus. We have both grown to love you, Wemaw and I. It would give us such joy if you would agree to be our son."

Lucas sat stunned. He couldn't move. He was so touched. "No one has ever wanted me before," he thought as he looked down at the table.

Grandpa broke the long silence with, "I know. We're old. You don't have to decide right…"

Lucas interrupted. "Are you sure?"

Wemaw grabbed his hand. "Yes, darlin', we are sure. In fact, we were heartbroken this week when we thought, well, never mind." Fighting back tears, she smiled sweetly. "Yes, we are sure. Will you be our son?"

He squeezed her hand tightly. "Yes, yes, I will!"

They gave celebratory hugs, all around. Afterward, Grandpa said, "Let's go see Mr. Phipps." On the way to Mr. Phipps, Lucas said, "Is there any way we could get rid of that grandfather clock? It creeps me out."

"Nope," said Grandpa with a smile. "You'll get used to it."

"Well, do I have to sleep upstairs?"

"Yes."

"Ok. Ok."

Meanwhile, Phil was driving Manny home as Manny was processing what Phil had just told him.

"He's going to be my uncle?"

"Yep. Yeah, Uncle Lucas, how do you like the sound of that?"

"Uncle Lucas? I can't believe it," said Manny, still bewildered.

Phil laughed out loud. "Amazing. God is good, Manny. God is good."

The family came together that night for another celebratory dinner. Across the table, Manny said, "Hello, Uncle."

"Hello, nephew."

Sammy laughed.

Lucas looked over at Manny after taking a bite of chicken. "Hey, you know… I am older than you. I didn't look after you like I should have in the orphanage, but that changes now, ok?"

Sammy chimed in. "Look out Manny. He wants to tell you what to do."

Manny looked at Sammy. "I think what he means is that he'll look out for me." He paused and continued, "Like a big brother."

"No, like an uncle!" Lucas teased. "You have to respect your elders."

TWO MONTHS LATER, the family gathered at the courthouse. Lucas's adoption hearing had come one week prior to his eighteenth birthday.

The court bailiff saw Grandpa standing in the hallway and approached him.

"Judge O'Connell, I have a question."

Grandpa smiled at him. "Yes, sir?"

"Well, I see that Judge Spavitz is conducting the adoption hearings today. Don't you usually conduct those hearings on Fridays?"

Grandpa's smile remained. "Sergeant, the State of Texas doesn't let a judge conduct his own adoption hearing."

Grandpa could see the confused look on the bailiff's face, so he further explained. "My wife and I are adopting a seventeen-year-old today. He's right over there." Grandpa pointed him out to the bailiff. "He's a good-looking boy, don't you think?"

The bailiff's jaw dropped, and his mouth stood agape for a half-second. He then slapped the judge's back while saying, "My, oh my. How wonderful! Congratulations, Judge O'Connell!"

"Thanks, Sergeant," said Grandpa, now walking toward his family and away from the bailiff. "Have a good Friday."

"You too, Judge. You too. I'm sure you will have a very good day."

The family sat down together in the courtroom. Lucas sat between Grandpa and Manny as they waited for the proceedings to begin. Sammy, Sarah, and Phil sat on the other side of Manny. Wemaw sat on the other side of Grandpa. The courtroom where justice is blind and terribly objective usually feels cold to visitors and participants. But on this occasion, the place felt warm and wonderful to the family.

While waiting, Lucas looked down, catching a glimpse of his new father's hand scar. He couldn't help tease his soon-to-be nephew seated next to him. Lucas whispered to Manny, "Judge Frankenstein? You know, you couldn't have been more wrong."

Manny whispered back, "Yes, I know. He's the best."

As Judge Spavitz entered the courtroom and began his comments, Manny smiled to himself. He then silently prayed to his Heavenly Father, "Thank You for this moment. You're the best. I couldn't have been more wrong about You."

24

A CLOCK AND A FRAME

On the following afternoon, Grandpa watched Lucas pull into the driveway. He walked out to greet his son and help him carry boxes from the car to his new room upstairs.

"Hi there, it was nice of Mr. Phipps to let you use the orphanage car one last time."

"He asked me to take it through the car wash before I return it."

Grandpa nodded and grabbed a box. The two men carried a box into the house through the back door and then walked through the dining room into the hallway. They passed by the large grandfather clock before ascending the stairs. After dropping off the boxes in Lucas' room, they descended the stairs as the grandfather clock struck 3 pm. At the base of the stairwell, Grandpa said, "Hey, Lucas, wait here just a second." The last of the three loud gongs faded into silence as they paused the move in process and stood near the ticking timekeeper.

"Lucas, I want to tell you something about this clock. I know Sammy and Manny are afraid of it."

"No, not really."

"Yes, they are. Anyway, I grew up with this clock, you see. My parents owned it when I was a boy, and they gave it to me long ago. I know it's loud and obnoxious, but the ticks, tocks, and gongs are familiar. They actually comfort me."

"Oh ok. I get that."

"Well, there's one more thing. Many years ago, I was hurt and had to spend several days in the hospital. Several days."

"Really, what happened to you?"

"I'll tell you about that some other time, or maybe Wemaw, I mean, your Mom will tell you. Actually, it's her I want to talk about."

"Ok."

"When I was in the hospital, I had lots of injuries that the doctors didn't want infected, so I was extremely limited on visitation. Basically, I was alone in the room trying to deal with my pain. It was no fun."

"Yikes. Sorry." Lucas gave him a pat.

"Your Mom knew I was suffering. She did something to help me that I'll never forget. She tape recorded the gurglings of this old clock on an old tape recorder. Do you know what that is? You may have seen one in a museum."

Lucas laughed. "Yes, I've seen them."

"She recorded the clock sounds for an hour and brought the tape and the tape player to my hospital room. During the remainder of my stay, I played the tape quite often. The clock sounds made me feel slightly more at home in that dark, lonely room."

"Wow, that was really nice of her."

"Her act of kindness toward me touched me so much that now, when I hear the clock…"

He paused to fight back emotion and then continued.

"When I hear the clock, I think of her. Does that make sense?"

"It does."

"Well, Sammy and Manny don't know that story. So, you can just let them spin their tales, and you will know they're full of it, ok?"

"Ha, yes, Dad. Ok."

~

ON THE FOLLOWING SATURDAY EVENING, Grandpa and Wemaw hosted a celebratory family dinner in their home. The boys hung out together while Phil and Sarah helped the hosts prepare the meal in the kitchen. At one point, Lucas passed by, and Sarah couldn't help herself. She greeted him.

"What's up, brother?"

He smiled back and gave her a wink.

As Phil took a bowl of mashed potatoes into the dining room, he set them down on the table. He then saw something that he had never seen before. There was a new wall-hanging that was large and prominent near the head of the table. Phil walked up to admire it. He stared at the words contained within the frame and they melted him.

"A Father to the fatherless, a defender of widows, is God in his holy dwelling,

God sets the lonely in families, he leads out the prisoners with singing."

Psalm 68:5-6

When Grandpa saw Phil return to the kitchen, he could see that he was moved. "Are you ok, Phil?" he said playfully.

"Yeah. That's really a beautiful scripture on the wall. The wood frame: I love it. Is that new?"

Wemaw overheard and interrupted. "That was Lucas' idea. He was quite insistent on it being displayed for all to see."

When Lucas sat down for dinner twenty minutes later,

the frame and its contents caught his eye. He read the words once more and took them in. He looked around the table. His table. His parents were talking to his sister, Sarah. His brother-in-law was telling a story to his nephews, who suddenly burst with laughter. Lucas absorbed it all. Overwhelmed in his heart, Lucas bowed his head for a moment and whispered, “Thank you, Father.”

ABOUT THE AUTHOR

Christopher D. Taylor is a retired judge who practiced law in Texas for twenty five years. In his retirement, he is compelled to shed light on the truth of God as revealed in Jesus Christ. Chris now lives in Southern California where his wife Maria of twenty-four years, was born and raised. Together they have two adult children.

www.ingramcontent.com/pod-product-compliance
Lightning Source LLC
Chambersburg PA
CBHW022056050726
47591CB00002B/569